# Donta Naughty

## Nathalie M.L. Römer

ISBN-13: 9789188459398



Emerentsia Publications
Marielundsvägen 9c
711 95 Gusselby
Sweden
emerentsiabooks.com


Ordering Information:

Orders by U.S. trade bookstores and wholesalers. Please contact Ingram: One Ingram Blvd., La Vergne, TN 37086   •   615.793.5000 or visit www.ingramcontent.com.

Independently printed as a Swedish publication.


Interior design and layout by Emerentsia Publications.

Official Website:
nathaliemlromer.com

Official Facebook Page:
facebook.com/nathaliemlromer

Official Twitter Account:
twitter.com/nathaliemlromer

Book website: nathaliemlromer.com/donta-naughty

# Donta Naughty

## Chapter One

Donta stares at the tavern's signage before he glances once more at a faded letter his second cousin had left behind a decade ago; weeks before setting off for his journey, which is *now* making him famous across the land. His second cousin's story is one of bravery and adventure. Donta wants the same…

He'd hoped to persuade his father's youngest servant to accompany him, but the servant had refused.

Profusely…

In the end, Donta set off alone - quietly and early so not to fall victim to the ridicule of the cook and the housemaids who always seem to come after him for more than just companionship.

"I guess this is it," he mumbles. Laughter greets his words coming from inside the inn; as if they were laughing at him. He feels his face heat.

"Fuck it. I'm hungry and if they're laughing at me, so be it," he says pointedly, having *no* real audience for the words, "And *you* can keep your thoughts to yourself…"

Donta looks down.

It's clear that one specific sound from within the tavern causes the feeling of embarrassment he now seems to experience.

He looks back up at the tavern's signage to scrutinise it once more. He opens the door a moment later, and it's the silence greeting him now that puts worry into his mind…

~~~

A sultry woman with long black hair stares at him. She smiles at the newcomer; she turns and grabs two large mugs from a shelf behind her. She calls out and a stocky man appears from a room beyond the bar. The man immediately scrutinises the newcomer, like every other person present is doing, seemingly. Donta feels his face becoming hotter. He's convinced the woman is scrutinising *one* specific part of him…
~~~

"You want beer?" she calls out, obviously aiming the question at Donta, "What's your name? All of us here know each other's names…"

Donta nods, tongue tied, and obviously blushing now.

She giggles.

It's one of those giggles he'd heard from the housemaids at home so often, causing him to cringe from the embarrassment he now feels.

A hand grabs his, and he's dragged towards the darkest corner of the tavern. He's pushed into the cushioned seating. They placed two mugs on the table between him and the woman sitting opposite him. He looks at her, and again is greeted by a sultry smile. A smile that seems to become irresistible as time passes.

*How long have I been here already?*

Donta pulls his gaze away from her and looks around the room. The man who appeared when she called out was leaning on the bar; his gaze direct and apparently studying him. He tries to smiles, but he's unsure if he did when the man frowns. Donta's gaze moves now towards the others in the tavern. Something seems wrong with the people present in the tavern around him…

His attention snaps back towards the woman when

she grips his hand and pulls him forward. He stares at her when he realises what she just did. He looks down, finding both his hands over her breasts, and his hand seemed to have taken over from his brain. They were squeezing her breasts - hard.

*What the fuck...*, Donta thinks.

He tries to pull away, but it seems she possesses an unnatural strength unlike any he'd ever encountered among any woman he'd met in his life. He repeats his actions.

"NO!"

Donta stares at the woman. The harshness of this singular word doesn't match the sultry nature of the smile present on her face. Again, the smile seems to draw him in, and this time, he tries to smile back at her...

"What's your name?" Donta blurts out.
"Carlotta."
"That's... a beautiful name," he says hesitantly, hoping that 'being nice' will diminish her grip on him; both in terms of her smile and the grip of her hands.
"And *you*?" she asks.
"Donta Quixote," he answers, "and they named me after my second cousin—We come from the family of la—"
"Hmm, boring. I'm going to call you Donta Naughty," she says before giggling incessantly. "You look like

someone who'd be naughty with a *girl* like me... Oh and don't mind *him*."

She nods towards the bar, and Donta follows her gaze to be met with an angry frown on the face of the man still standing there.

"Who is he?" he asks.

"My father," she answers. "He might like none of this going on, but he has no hold over me at all. Don't you, father...?"

Donta stares back at Carlotta. Her face now had a chiselled appearance, like she could be one of the marble statues he'd seen in the last town he passed through before arriving at this small tavern. Something was off about how she's behaving, and now he's aware of her behaviour, it's clear that every person in the tavern was acting similarly all of them were acting with a similar coldness, and all were staring at him now.

"Let me GO..." Donta hisses, "I'm certain this is the wrong tavern. I hoped to get to the tavern that my cousin had visited."

"NO!"

Donta stares angrily at Carlotta when she spits out this word once more and seems to pull him closer to herself. She smiles, and Donta kisses her lips. He rips away from the woman just moments later, and wipes his mouth with the one arm he had freed.

"So, you don't like being kissed by a girl?" she says, "Maybe one of them could kiss you instead…"
Donta sees her nudge her head towards him. A moment later, a man sits beside Donta. He glances at the man, and is met by a smirk.
"No, no, no. I don't mind you kissing me…" Donta protests.

Finding her lips on his once more makes it clear Carlotta had grabbed hold of his arm once more, and when he glances down, it's obvious now what she did while the man next to distracted him…

# Chapter Two

Donta feels wetness on his hand where it had been pushed underneath Carlotta's skirt. He's uncertain who's the culprit, but he guesses it is Carlotta, who's now sitting on the table, one of her legs on either side of him, and who seemed to enjoy his discomfort.

Donta attempts to pull his hand back, but realises fast that another hand - much stronger than his own - keeps his hand in place. It seems the man beside him is assisting in Carlotta's attempts to force him into pleasuring her.

Donta frowns, as it's clear that she has an unexplained power over *that* part of his body.

Her hand is doing a similar pleasuring of him, it

# Donta Naughty

seems…

*It seems—What the fuck is going on? Where am I? Who is she? Why is her father not pulling her away and kicking me out of here…?*

She kisses him again, and this time he feels her bare nipple under his other hand. The confused thoughts disappear from his mind. The urge to do more to her and with her grows by the minute. She isn't one of the coy house maids he's used to. She seems to exude passion. Lots and lots of it. And *not* the sort he'd previously encountered.

Before today, the only time they had ever invited him to a bed was by sheer force of presence, always using his famous connections with his cousin as a means of persuasion. Carlotta didn't know or didn't care about who he was or what his family ties were.

*Donta Naughty… hmm, it sounds odd, but it sounds appropriate in an odd sort of way,* Donta thinks. *Perhaps there's my career of fame to be had with such a name…*

A groan…

*Did I groan, or did she? Who is she anyway?*

Another groan, more high-pitched this time.

*That was her this time. She'd better not stop this. It's so much*

# Donta Naughty



*better than—*

Donta frowns as he realises that he's treating this as one of his conquests in bed, but he isn't the conqueror here.

*She's doing all the conquering. She's seducing me. She's making me the target of her sexual desires. But the question is, how the fuck is she doing this? She said that's her father. She's making him watch all of this—somehow. She's making this guy beside me participate, too.*

"What the hell are you doing to me?" he asks.

Carlotta simply smiles, but in the next moment she pushes his hand away.

*Damn, damn, damn,* Donta thinks, letting out a grunt of frustration.

Carlotta laughs out loud, taunting his mind even more. He feels frozen in place, similar to her father's stance, as she buttons up and re-adjusts her petticoat back into its normal position. Another few blinks later and she sits again opposite him... *at* the table rather than on top of it.

Donta glances around, confused, when everyone in the tavern talks again. Her father talks to the patron to his left. The patrons seated around them lean in and continue whatever conversation they had been having before they had become frozen in place. The grip loosens from his arm and it's gone a moment later.

# Donta Naughty

It all takes a matter of seconds, yet everything feels like it takes an eternity. Donta stares back at Carlotta, who seems to get amusement from the situation he finds himself in and he doesn't share it…

***

"DO you want a drink? My father's gin is the best in the province…" Carlotta swoons at Donta like she's simply a tavern keeper's daughter, and not the wild creature from minutes before.

Donta hesitates answering the question.

"DO you want a drink?" she repeats.

He nods quickly because her sharp outburst causes several heads to turn.

"You don't have to be such a bitch…" Donta whispers.

"Did I hear you right?" Carlotta screams.

Donta pushes away from her as far as the table and seating will allow him to go. He stares at her wide-eyed.

"Let me get one thing straight—bitch," Carlotta says menacingly. "When YOU get offered a woman's fruit you do *not* disregard it with such contempt… Do you understand me?"

Donta nods hastily.

"Now, stay sitting here and I'll bring back the gin. He—" she says, pointing with a finger at the man beside

Donta. "He'll make sure you STAY… Do you understand me?"

Another nod.

Carlotta rises, and after staring at Donta for several minutes, she turns and walks to the bar. She makes swift work of pouring out four stoneware mugs with gin and after handing one cup to her father, she returns with the other mugs.

She sits and pushes a mug in front of Donta and another in front of the man beside Donta, who nods and rises and walks off, but not too far.

"He knows he cannot be listening to what I'm going to talking about next with you—" Carlotta grunts before she drinks up all her gin. Donta expects her words to come out like a slurred mess when she speaks again. "I have a proposal for you. I doubt a strapping man would refuse an offer from a pretty girl like myself…"

"It depends on the proposal…" Donta grunts under his breath, feeling on his guard now. He backs away, just in case she screams again, but she simply smiles.

*Something about her constant smiling is putting me off her,* Donta thinks with scepticism entering his mind. *Something tells me I will not be allowed to say no to whatever she's proposing. Maybe I can string her along for a while. It won't hurt me to find out what this proposal might be… Maybe, she's in danger and she was just forcing me to take part to throw the culprit off…*

"I'm listening…" Donta says neutrally.

"There's this matter I need to attend to," Carlotta purrs. "It's a matter *they* cannot know about, you see. It's a delicate matter… I'd guess a noble soul *would* assist a girl in need…"

Donta smirks at the comment and gets ready for whatever she's going to tell him next.

# Chapter Three

As he waits for Carlotta to continue, Donta realises fast it may be the first time in his life that *any* person has called him a 'noble soul.' He knows words are much more appropriate for his famous second cousin who he only shares a last name with, so he asks, "So I'm a noble soul, huh?"

She nods fervently.

He adds, "And you need help with something, huh?"

Another nod, but it's followed quickly by another one of her smirks she'd shown a few times already and his eyebrows knot closer, feeling caution for what she *may* tell him, what the quest for him to fulfil might be...

# Donta Naughty

"I belong to… well, it doesn't matter, really, what I might belong to… They *need* me for an event and they—" Carlotta says but she stops in mid-sentence, and instead her face broadens into a glorious grin. A genuine grin this time rather than the half-hearted smirk she'd shown up to now.

"You can tell me…" Donta quips.

"Alright…" Carlotta says. "There is… a society. That's the best way I can explain it. I need to bring a guest… That's about it."

"So you need a chaperon?" Donta asks.

"Hmm, if you want to put it that way… errr… yes, that's right?" she answers. The answer comes hastily and insincerely. Donta ignores that part of her answer. He wants to be as famous as his famous cousin.

*Maybe this is my chance to be a hero…*

"Yes, I guess I need a chaperon…" Carlotta whispers, and leaning forward she adds, "Or perhaps you do, Donta Naughty…"

"My name isn't—" Donta snaps.

"I know, I know… It's so hilarious to see a hero be offended so easily by a bit of teasing… or get a hard-on so easily when I show these…"

Donta grunts loudly when he feels a stiffening in his loins, and he grumbles under his breath, "Dammit…"

Carlotta laughs loudly as she readjusts her clothing back into place, and she calmly adds, "I guess these hold sway over you more than I'd ever imagined…"

"But… I want to help you with whatever troubles you…"

Donta tries to fill his words with the same confidence he'd heard his famous cousin speak with whenever he's asked to relate to one of his many adventures.

"Before I tell more, I want you to understand you cannot tell anyone about it. Not my father, not anyone here, not your family…" she says.

A fleeting frown before he nods.

"Swear you won't tell a soul… I want to hear you say it," she hisses.

"Alright, alright… I swear on my grandmother's grave that I won't tell any person what you'll tell me…" Donta hisses back.

"Hmm, your grandmother, huh? Was *she* special to you?" she asks bluntly.

He nods.

"I guess that will do…" she says, and she pulls out a small parchment from a pocket in her skirt, "It seems I've fulfilled almost all the requirements the… society… calls for…."

"Tell me more about this society?" Donta asks cautiously.

"It's a gathering for choosing the new vampire leadership," she answers tersely.

"It—is—what…?" Donta asks. For a moment, he wasn't certain he heard the words correctly.

"I said: IT is a society of vampires. I WANT to be

considered for its leadership. YOU will make it happen," she says with coldness dripping from every word.

"How?" Donta hisses. "How can I make 'what' happen?"

"By being my… chaperon," she purrs once more.

"Is that all?" he asks. "It's not anything else?"

She shakes her head. Donta believes her… for now, at least.

"What else do you need to do still?" he asks. "It seems you have a list…"

"So, you're okay with *them* being vampires?" she counters.

"I don't believe they exist. The village I grew up in has many stories of them…" he answers. "All of them end with it going badly for the people who involve themselves with them."

For a moment Donta sees fear in Carlotta's eyes, and she narrows her eyes and asks, smiling maliciously, "For the person involving themselves or for their 'dinner'…?"

"Dinner? Do vampires eat dinner…?"

"Of course they do… How else do they stay looking young and voluptuous…"

Carlotta pushes her breasts up, so to point them at Donta's face and when, in response to the words spoken, he blanches she smiles.

He realises *he* might be 'dinner.' Her words imply it as much.

"I guess I've explained it enough for you to understand what I mean," Carlotta says sharply. "There's *no* need for you to know the finer details…"

"Why not?" Donta asks angrily. "It's a matter of honour for *you* to be truthful about your intentions…"

"Why should I have to prove myself?" she hisses. "I'd like to know what your intentions were when you arrived here. Is the supposed famous cousin even real…?"

"He is, and he did many great deeds…" Donta protests.

"So why are you here instead of him?" Carlotta spits out. "I want a hero for my quest, not some downtrodden nobody who—"

"I'm *not* a nobody…" Donta yells. "I will help you with your quest, but only if you stop this incessant behaviour of either finding fault *or* trying to seduce me…"

Carlotta appears momentarily like she's about to hit back with a renewed salvo of reasons to object, but after a minute of silence she leans back, grabs hold of the mug with a few drops of gin and downs it. She just stares hard at the man opposite her with her face contorting in anger.

Carlotta's frown shows to Donta to stay silent.

Very, very silent.

Donta notes his outburst has altered Carlotta's demeanour entirely. First she frowns; she stares at him angrily; and moments later, her contemptuous smile is back. The annoying smirk which seems to draw him in, and within a few seconds he feels like he should touch her breasts…

# Chapter Four

Donta slowly takes his gaze off her face - and her body she's flaunting purposely. Instead, he stares at the floor, which increasingly becomes the focus of his attention. As he stares, he imagines patterns. Lots of patterns resembling shapes. And the shapes are moving, it seems…

As they move, they take on imagery from the stories he'd heard about his more famous cousin and he thinks, *Damn you, Donta, all this for a bit of glory like him. What's really going on here? Is she in some sort of danger and is her anger staged to mask her plea for help? I need to find out… somehow…*

"Tell me what's going on?" Donta asks sternly. He feels surprise at the demanding tone in his voice. He'd never spoken in this way to any woman ever in his life, remembering the scolding he received from his mother a decade earlier for this behaviour towards his younger sister.

"What if I don't want to explain it? What if I want you to come with me, and will help me with…?" Carlotta snaps. "Why do the heroes of stories always *need* some sort of explanation of the quest to help with, like they lack the intelligence to figure out to simply help…"

"Fine. Don't explain it," Donta responds. "But it will make it less likely that I'll help you…"

"Hmm, that's rude…" Carlotta spits out.

"Not as rude as telling someone they lack intelligence…" he snaps back.

For several minutes, they silently glare at one another, each hoping to win the battle of will over the other person.

"So, are you telling me about your troubles, or not?" Donta snaps once more.

"Fine, fine, I'll tell you a bit. The rest would bore you to sleep anyway," Carlotta grunts. "But first, I want to know more about you. Why are you travelling? Where are you going?"

"I'm on my way to the west coast, to one city there, to board a ship," Donta answers after he stares intently for a minute at the woman who seems to match his facial expressions, "I want to see more of the world. I want to be an explorer…"

Carlotta looks down at the floor beside the table, and she laughs out loud and says, "With only one bag? It sounds more like you grabbed a few belongings quickly and left your home telling no one where you were going. With ONE bag in your possession, you sound more like a little boy who ran away from home because he didn't like something his father told him."

"So what if I left with only one bag…" Donta grunts, folding his arms across his chest defensively.

It's clear to him that Carlotta is out to make fun of him as much as most of the female servants of his father would do.

"I guess you've also brought a mighty sack full of gold coins with you that hides in this bag. Am I right?" Carlotta continues taunting. "Maybe I should get one of them to check your bag for me…"

"No!" Donta shouts angrily. "Why can't you leave me alone."

"And end up without some fun…? Not a chance…" Carlotta says icily.

"Hmm, you know you're a damned bitch," Donta grunts.

"So are *you*…" Carlotta says, and she laughs loudly at Donta's shocked face, before she continues speaking in hushed tones, "… but my quest *will* be much more fun than this boring journey you've planned for yourself. Aren't you even the slightest bit interested in rescuing a maiden like that—hmm, well, I have to guess that you're Donta Naughty even more if you ran away from home?"

"Hmm, so I guess I'll have to put up with you calling me that name…"

"If you're offended by a name, you're not much of a hero…" Carlotta says. "I doubt a proper hero minds the comments they might get about their lives."

"Well, if we're going to be discussing this in terms of characters from a story then—" Donta says. He pauses before he adds, "… in most of the stories there is always someone seducing the hero and he or she is usually the bad person…"

"Oh, so I'm bad? Is that what you claim about me when you know nothing about me…" Carlotta snaps before glancing - more worried than should have been the case - towards her father standing unmoving at the bar.

"Did he cause your worry?" Donta asks after also glancing at the old man.

"NO!"

Donta jumps at the force in Carlotta's voice. "We will not talk about him or to him… Do you understand me?"

Donta nods sheepishly. Then it takes all his willpower to glance over once again at the man who'd been introduced as this woman's father. But he realises already that something is definitely wrong here even if he cannot determine or how.

It had been a curiosity for knowing more about a wider world that had driven Donta from his home. In that, Carlotta was correct. But now, weeks later, it was something else that was stirring additional curiosity. Who exactly is this woman? Why does she show such animosity towards her father? What is the nature of the quest she's seeking help with? Why is there something so unworldly about her behaviour that seems to draw him in making her so damned irresistible…?

~~~
~~~

# Donta Naughty

Donta almost spits out his beer when Carlotta sits again beside him, and she places her arm gently around his shoulders.

"Are you interested in a party?" Carlotta asks, smirking maliciously.

"Party?" Donta asks.

"Yes, a party… I want you to come with me," she answers. "I'm supposed to bring someone with me. It's organised for ten days from now."

"I hadn't planned to stay here for ten days. I want to be at—" Donta protests.

"You WILL stay here because I said so…" Carlotta hisses. "I want you to help me because I said so…"

Donta blushes, and for an unknown reason he can't even raise his voice in protest after this latest outburst from Carlotta…

# Chapter Five

Donta shivers uncontrollably when two fingers slide softly over the still boyish skin of his lower belly. He'd grown hairs on this part of his body that, perhaps, one day, would resemble the bushy chest hair of his father. But not yet. At twenty years old, he still resembles a boy more than a man.

"Stop it…" Donta squeals, immediately cursing inwardly for sounding more like a boy in this moment of passion with the mysterious daughter of a tavern keeper. But three days in bed and to be privy to endless sex with someone who isn't even protesting whenever he asks for more has never been an option, Donta has considered as closing the front door of his home ever so quietly.

# **Donta Naughty**

"Stop… what?" Carlotta asks, and immediately her fingers are tracing slowly towards Donta's belly button. She leans closer so one breast touches his skin.

It causes a reaction from him.

Donta grunts loudly when he feels the reaction happens in his loins. This somewhat playful activity to get him to get an erect penis had become a game for Carlotta, and she immediately smiles at him; warmly and invitingly, yet the smile feels like torture to him.

Part of his mind *wants* to enjoy this activity, however the feeling of dread grows as the activity never stops; especially whenever they're in the tavern, which causes him to protest just a slight bit louder each time Carlotta persists with her behaviour towards him. In his younger years of just three years earlier, Donta saw men force themselves onto women, even when such a woman would say 'no.' This is the *first* time they had subjected him to a situation of a woman being forceful in the matters of sex. Carlotta is the one in a position of power regarding anything that resembles a sexual activity, rather than him being the one to start such activities…

*Why me?* Donta's mind despairs as the days drag on. *Why did I get myself into this stupid situation?*

He had been told the event that Carlotta needs help with was due to happen in ten days from today. She wasn't forthcoming in terms of any other detail.

# Donta Naughty

When Carlotta moves her hand away from Donta's belly to start slowly tracing his stomach once more, he reaches out and for the first time since the activities had begun, he grabs hold of her wrist firmly and stops her behaviour.

"NO!" he shouts. "I said for you to stop this ridiculous behaviour…"

"Ah, so there's a *man* hidden in this body," she hisses maliciously. "I guess I might as well lie on my back with my legs spread for you to have your way with me…"

"I hadn't ever planned anything like that," he says firmly. "All I wanted was for you to STOP your behaviour right now. If you don't like it when I protest against your behaviour—what makes you think I *would* like it… huh?"

Carlotta is silent. She refuses to answer his demand and her face shows the dismay over being forced to consider this sudden question. At least at first, and because Donta stays quiet, she's forced to consider the implications of her actions.

After a few minutes, she shrugs her shoulders, and she quietly says, "I guessed you'd be like all others. That it is alright to grab a girl, and have your way with her… I thought I'd give you a bit of your own medicine…"

"I might have tempted girls or women to have sex with me, but I always asked her *first* if she wanted it…" Donta grunts.

"Are you telling me I'm *not* the first…?" Carlotta asks,

now with genuine surprise in her voice. "I thought—"

"You thought wrong. And NO, I will not dishonour the girls or women I've been with before I met you by telling you who they are and what we did…" Donta snaps.

Carlotta grunts, and she rolls to her back abruptly.

Donta sighs relief that, rather unexpectedly, he'd cut short the 'game' between them. She's silent, staring at the ceiling with a chiselled expression on her face. It's obvious to Donta that she doesn't like what she heard him say. The boot, as they say, is on the other foot now in terms of the dimension of their volatile emerging relationship.

A hesitant hand touches Donta's arm. He glances sidelong, and frowns at Carlotta's glazed eyes.

"I need to go downstairs to help Father," she whispers. "I heard him call out for me…"

Donta frowns and is curious how she could hear her father when he couldn't.

"Can we talk later, and I will tell you everything," she says. "You stay here and when I'm back we'll talk about what I want to do…"

"It's not like I can go anywhere without wearing my clothes… huh!" Donta grunts. "Proves that you don't trust me…"

Donta frowns deeply as Carlotta simply walks from the room and laughs out loud. Again, like in the last ten days, she omits to tell him where his clothes are located.

# Donta Naughty

~~~

Donta drops his head back on the pillow, exhaling. As much as he wants to understand Carlotta, he cannot. He realises there's a darkness about her that made her the way she was. He shakes his head, feeling dismayed, then glances down his naked body and grunts loudly. The evidence of her pleasuring was visible as a long protruding sexual organ that throbbed with the rhythm of his heartbeat and he didn't like how exposed he feels because of his 'situation' which comprised finding all of his clothing, including the spare clothing in his haversack, all having vanished the morning after his first night of sleep in one of the smallest bed chambers of the tavern the furthest from the front of the building used by the patrons.

He sighs, drops his head back down once more, then frustration causes him to growl loudly. It's obviously moments later that Carlotta is true to her words of being able to hear stuff when he hears her annoying laughter answer his frustration. She'd heard him curse, and like previous days, she makes certain that he knows it...
~~~

# Chapter Six

Donta lays his head back down after glancing up for fifth time. It seems Carlotta isn't coming back immediately despite saying she would before she'd left him. At least *not* today...

Donta frowns and wonders if there's another reason for her absence.

He shakes his head and wrinkles his face into a frown of frustration and a bit of disgust. The reactionary emotions the situation evokes relate more to his own reaction to behaviour that's so common to the society he lives in, where a divide exists between those with wealth and those subservient to the wealthy. He realises now how privileged he'd been at home, and that leaving the comfort of his abode had forced him into a situation where he was being confronted with how different things are for the lower classes. Something about Carlotta's situation odd to him, like she might be capable of being part of his circle of society, yet she was in a situation of obvious poverty…

*I need to figure out something about her situation, and her specifically*, Donta decides after a few minutes of silently contemplating. *Something else is wrong here. Her reaction was not the behaviour of someone happy to leave. What's up with her father, anyway? Maybe she wants to leave. I remember about Dulcinea that her life wasn't that happy before my cousin arrived. Did I arrive at a similar situation by accident?*

Donta lifts from the bed and walks to the window. He needs to relief himself, and although his next actions were more common among the common folk that are employed by his father, the lack of clothing would make it impossible for him to venture outside the room.

He opens the window and leans out to check for anyone in the fields or closer to the tavern. At the window, the murmur of voices from the tavern is audible, but he cannot make out what's said. He listens specifically for a familiar laughter, but Carlotta doesn't seem to have a reason to feel cheerful.

He straightens up and takes hold of his penis and aims it at the open window.

A wry smile appears on his face as he watches the arc

of clear yellow fluid disappear to the ground below the window, and he realises now why some menfolk at his father's estate would laugh so much if they managed to time it with precision for it to soak an unfortunate servant girl or stable boy in the stink of their urine. He now hopes the liquid coats the man who'd forced him into the actions of a forced sexual encounter with Carlotta, and would walk into the tavern and get a salvo of laughter for the ridicule of being in such a situation.

A few shakes, and he's done with relieving himself. He turns and almost expects Carlotta to be standing at the doorway with her hands positioned on her hips. Another part of him hopes she'd even had returned and quietly undressed herself and be waiting for him to turn…

But he's alone.

He sighs deeply, walks to the bed, and flops down hard on the mattress with a measure of frustration in his actions. He cringes when his spine meets the hard surface of the straw below the thin mattress. Again, a sign of how different this world outside his sheltered life at his father's mansion was, even if his father was not among the most affluent or influential of his family.

The measure of wealth that existed in his family had come from Quixote's pursuits; both the early ones in which he'd met and taken home with him, the beautiful and enigmatic Dulcinea, but the greater wealth came from the fame that spread later. Stories were conjured up about fantastical adventures that Quixote might, or might not, have done. Each was more fantastical than the previous. There were scholars who asked for Quixote on matters of literature and included variations of his adventures in books. And they'd pay a hefty gold purse to Quixote.

The wealth eventually spread to other branches of the extended family, though not in a great measure as Donta's father wanted, which he'd curse about many a night when another week would go by without an envoy with sacks of gold from Quixote…

"He's not as generous as he wants the public to know," Donta grunts under his breath. "I doubt I'd even would have left home if he shares more of his wealth. But, somehow, Father always had enough wealth to gain influence…"

"What the hell are you mumbling about?"

Donta frowns, more from his thought process being interrupted than from the obvious curious tone in Carlotta's voice. She smirks when he stares at him.

"I was contemplating my reasons for even leaving my home in the first place…" Donta confesses. He is brutally honest with Carlotta in case this might elicit answers from her about her own identity. She frowns for just a moment then says with all possible insolence in her voice, "… and I guess you want to go to daddy, right? He's some sort of hero to you, right?"

# Donta Naughty

"Actually... no," Donta replies. "I hate him with a passion. He's opposed every plan I ever had since I was just five years old. He wants me to be the token puppet 'owner' of his estate when he's an invalid. He said just three days before I left that if I left, I better not come back unless I come home with a suitable bride blessed by the padre on my arm. He said that if he approves of her, he'd give me half my inheritance there and then and that I could then do whatever I want with the rest of my life. If I find such a person I'll just take her home for a few days, get the inheritance, then go to the Americas as planned..."

Donta realises quickly that this wasn't the answer Carlotta had expected when her smirk goes from faintly friendly to the malicious smirk she'd carried on the first night at the tavern...

"Oh, right," she says coldly. "But I guess my plans change all that..."

# Chapter Seven

For several minutes, they lock their gazes in a test of whose willpower is stronger than that of the other individual. After a few minutes of this happening, Carlotta's smile vanishes, and she simply reaches down and lifts her skirt up. When she's upright once more, with a massive bundle of her clothing in front of her belly, she grins broadly and invitingly at him.

"I guess you don't want more of this then…" she says before laughing loudly at the curse that escapes Donta's lips. His reaction is caused more by how his naked body reacts to seeing her nakedness.

"Were you in the tavern with your father without dressing yourself properly?" he asks.

"Why not… you didn't mind the benefits at your

arrival," she answers, swooning at Donta while encouraging his body to react further by inserting two fingers into her vagina. To him it's obvious she's pleasuring herself in that moment when a loud groan escapes involuntarily from her lips, that part ever so slightly as her actions increase.

He's on his feet when a second, louder groan escapes from her lips. He lifts Carlotta into his arms and has her carried to the bed in six heartbeats. He's on top of her, gripping her arms above her head. In a single thrust, he's inside her. As he pulls his stiff organ out, she groans loudly, and a moment later she gasps loud as he re-enters deeply.

Her moans become louder and more frequent, which causes Donta to speed up his own motions. He lets out a loud groan of his own when his sperm explodes into Carlotta's vagina. He's spent and sprawls on top of the woman who teases him with squeezes of the muscles of her female organ he didn't know women possess. It surprises him when even more sperm escapes his penis that's now fast becoming flaccid once more; even if this is happening inside Carlotta's vagina and she's now discovering a new way to tease him.

But a way of teasing that interestingly is giving him satisfaction and pleasure.

Amazingly, Carlotta is allowing herself to stay pinned under his body, and she's letting him keep her hands pinned up against the pillows of the bed with him gripping her wrists. She even seems to relax her body to give him a few moments of dominance over *her*. It surprises Donta she'd behave in this different way compared to how she'd been treating him in the preceding weeks when instead, she'd been definitely in charge.

Donta lowers his head to kiss Carlotta's shoulder; he also does this so she cannot see the surprised expression that's likely settled on his face over her behaviour. Kissing her neck causes him to feel a renewed wave of lusting for lovemaking to well up deep inside him; usually he was spent after having sex with a woman once, but not so with Carlotta. He feels his penis - which amazingly is still deep inside her - stiffening once again. It's obvious she notices it too as she sways her hips back and forth, although he can only guess what she may think right now of his more dominant male behaviour towards her.

He lifts his head ever so slightly and glances sidelong at her. *Her lips are curled into a playful, radiant smile. She's enjoying this. Maybe I should continue this for as long as possible…*

He kisses Carlotta's lips. She responds to the tenderness of his kiss. There is genuine passion in her response. She's enjoying their lovemaking. In fact, her response to his actions was filled with more passion than any other woman he'd laid with in the earlier years of his life whenever he'd indulged in such pursuits.

*Earlier in my life is just the last four or five years*, he thinks, smirking inwardly.

He kisses her forehead, then the tip of her nose that causes her to giggle like a small child. At the same time, her womanhood causes her to squeeze tightly around his manhood that's still deep inside her. Donta glances at her in response; she cocks her head playfully in response, showing merriment in her facial expressions.

*She's enjoying this*, he thinks.

With renewed hunger he kisses her red lips few dozen times, unable to kerb his passion. Now, his lovemaking became hurried, almost like an act of despair; like he may never have such a chance ever again.

*Perhaps, not if her plan - her quest - is going to be dangerous*, he thinks gleefully. *Whatever the quest may be... wherever it takes me. I'll please her... whatever it takes for me...*

The unexpected thought surprises him.

He pushes up, and for a few minutes looks down at the woman. Her eyes are closed. He pushes deep inside her to prevent her from opening her eyes. He didn't want her to question his puzzled gaze down at her, so he leans down and firmly places his lips over hers. He pushes his tongue into her mouth and at the same time, his essence explodes inside her womanhood.

She moans loudly...

# Donta Naughty

Donta drops spent on top of the woman and pants loudly. He has a hard time remembering any previous intercourse that was as intense as it was today with Carlotta. She was a willing participant, but the lovemaking was done on her terms. He knew she has the strength to push him away from her as it had happened a few times in the last ten days.

*Has it been that long already?* he thinks, frowning somewhat. He sets his facial features to neutral before he lifts his head once more and studies Carlotta's placid features. Her eyes are still closed. There's a mellow smile. She's breathing lightly. But the pinkness of her cheeks shows that she's still in a heightened euphoria from the lovemaking.

Donta sighs a moment, then he quickly rolls over and lies on his back, staring aimlessly at the ceiling above. Any moment her hand will torment him once again with her incessant hand jobs. They were tiring him. Her odd behaviour of being condescending and aloof was annoying him.

*If only I could persuade her somehow that being nice is better, but who am I to talk in this way when I've never been nice to any woman in my entire life...*

## Chapter Eight

The moonlight streaming in through the open window wasn't what woke Donta. It was a chilly breeze that woke him. He glances around, half expecting to be alone, but he sees Carlotta sleeping beside him, and for once her features show her mind to be at peace.

He frowns and studies her face for a few minutes before rising from the bed in a single silent motion. He smirks while pouring out his urine from the open window once more, then grins broadly when a curse comes from below. Someone was in the courtyard and he was being subjected to the piss coming from above.

Instead of looking down through the window to discover who might be at ground level below his window,

# Donta Naughty

Donta just shrugs his shoulders and walks back to the bed. He stands beside the bed with his legs spread apart, and if Carlotta wakes up, she'd be greeted by his manhood right beside her face. He stares down at her, and then his grin broadens further when he realises their situation is now reversed to his advantage. Rather than *she* being in charge of their situation, the roles are now reversed. He didn't know for how long this would go on, but for a while he could enjoy it.

*If she wakes and grabs my penis, that's actually good. That will teach her how I felt on the first night when she forced me to hold her breasts*, he thinks.

In the moonlight, Carlotta almost takes the serenity of one of the Madonna statues in the church near his home. *Why am I thinking so much about home all of a sudden?* Donta ponders. *It's not like any of them are going to miss me…*

He knows that, in reality, no one will miss a spoilt, sullen man who'd made it a sport to find himself in bed with as many of the servants of his father's household as he could manage in a day.

His shameful opinion, throughout his life as a boy transitioning from a boy to a man, had always been: because it's the done thing among all men that he *should* join in as well.

Falling in love with someone had always been the furthest from his mind. He expected the same to be true, right now…


*But why does my heart beat faster whenever Carlotta smiles at me, even when she does it for malicious reasons?*
This thought surprises Donta.

He studies Carlotta closer and realises that, for the first time in his life, he'd met someone who could be a suitable love interest and someone he wanted to be with for the rest of his days in this world. *Can I fall in love with someone with her behaviour or status? Should I even try to fall in love with her…?*


~~~


I't's when the moon has shifted towards a downward slope hours before the sun is due to rise that Carlotta wakes up and she's indeed is startled by Donta standing so close to her with his penis just a few inches from her face. Her eyes widen, then she stares up at the man standing next to the bed with his arms folded over his chest and staring coldly down at her.

"I guess you don't like it much when you're at the receiving end of such foul behaviour," he grunts before turning and sitting down in the chair near the open window. They stare at one another angrily; each having their own reasons to be in a sullen mood. This time, Donta doesn't look away, and after a few minutes it forced Carlotta to glance down by the fear that settles on her face.
~~~

# Donta Naughty

Donta frowns momentarily and for just a few seconds he feels compelled to ask what she's fearful about, but he holds his tongue. Silence is now his weapon to get *her* to confess her intentions and to tell him what's going on. He waits…

*One thing is certain, and that's that she's definitely afraid. Of what? Who? Why…?*

Hesitantly, almost cautiously, Donta reaches out to Carlotta's chin and pushes against it to force her to look him in the eye. Her eyes are glazed, but he also sees some tightness of her lips and a shallow frown on her forehead. She wasn't just upset. Something or someone was causing her to feel a seething anger that she kept under control.

*Something happened to her that caused her behaviour to become this way. Someone caused her harm. I guess that's what the quest she mentioned may be about…*

Without outright asking her why she's in this sullen mood, there wouldn't be any chance for him to find out what was really going on. If something was indeed going on. What is clear to him is that she wasn't simply using pretence as a weapon.

"Tell me…" he says plainly.

After a few moments of hesitation, she nods, then in a flat voice, she relates more of the details that had prompted her behaviour towards him.

"I'm trying to change something," she says. "In a society where even as a creature of the night, as a vampire you matter little when you're just a woman—I want to change all that by becoming—I want to have some control over what happens to me…"

"Hmm, in the end we're just all servants of God…" Donta grunts.

"I guess some padre said that to you… I heard… errr… I was told the same by… errr… some nuns. Never mind who they were, but they said similar," Carlotta says. "But since this has happened to me, it proves there's no one looking out for us from some higher place or he wouldn't let something like this happen to an innocent girl at the start of her adult life…"

"WHO did this to you?" he asks.

"It doesn't matter," she answers flatly. "But if I can get a position of leadership secured among the council, I can make changes."

"Council?"

"That's what they call themselves…" she answers. "It's the eldest of them who makes up the council. I want to change *that* too…"

# Chapter Nine

For several seconds, Donta stares puzzled at Carlotta. He *still* doesn't know what's going on in this tavern; in the region where the tavern is located; with the people of this region; but at least he has a few details hinting at *more* to come in terms of *her* quest.

She voiced exactly what's happening around him in the world.

He knows she's right when she said that women aren't valued in society. Even in her undead state as a vampire, this seems to be the case; maybe even more so.

To realise that *her* situation hadn't improved upon becoming a vampire does ultimately comes as a surprise to him.

# Donta Naughty

As she speaks from time to time - getting the information from her was as tedious as watching someone to do a bloodletting procedure on a sick man - Carlotta reveals a small clue about what her 'quest' is; though the details given to increase the mystery. His frown deepens to an angry scowl when the realisation of what she's hinting at sets in. She targeted him for a way to avenge for what she perceives as 'everything wrong' with the world—with *her* world. With her world as a woman…

Another part of Donta's mind considers the situation to be amusing, and he feels his lips push up into a wry smile. *Why do I find it all so amusing when it isn't amusing…?*

"Carlotta, are you trying to tell me something that happened to you?" he asks gently. His voice is much gentler than he expects it to be.

No response, and she looks away, and he sees her sighing deeply. He wishes now that he could read her mind. But alas, such was not the ability of a mortal man such as he…

Donta cranes his neck to see whether he can see any emotion - anger or otherwise - on Carlotta's face. She's biting her lip, and he's uncertain why she's doing this behaviour that usually was construed as a sign of weakness of the mind. *But her mind isn't weak…*

"Carlotta…" he mumbles as he places a hand on her

shoulder and pulls her upper body so she faces him. "Carlotta, TELL me what's going on…"

She shakes her head as an answer; the action has the air of desperation to it that doesn't fit with her previous behaviour of aloofness and pride. It's almost like she's changing in personality right in front of his eyes and although her previous behaviour of mastery over his emotions was annoying, this behaviour was even more so. And not for the same reasons…

"What is going on, Carlotta?" he asks with added urgency in his voice. He sits down next to Carlotta, knowing full well she could simply pretend to be in a sullen mood and use this moment to assert her power over him. He was sitting down naked beside her and she'd previously used this to her advantage. But, rather than pouncing onto his manhood as she's done so often before this moment, she turns further away from him like she's ashamed…

*Ashamed? HOW is she ashamed of what she did to me?*

~~~

Donta had felt momentary relief when Carlotta finally reacted in her usual demeanour to his accusation, even though he risked much by voicing his criticism of her behaviour so openly. Even if meant she was once again as mean and manipulative as weeks ago, he would coax the
~~~

truth about who she is and what she's dealing with. But something is different about her behaviour now compared to how it had been—even with the incessant giggling that had her in its grip now. But the giggles sound forced, and every word spoken between the snorts of more laughter sound forced.

*Like she isn't enjoying it anymore…*

He's surprised when she gets up, and then leaves the bedroom abruptly. She's back in the bedroom after several minutes holding a tight bundle of clothing in her hands.

His clothes…

She throws the clothing in his direction, and he only catches it by chance; he has to scramble to uncover his head and left shoulder from the clothing. He stares at her, surprised. She just shrugs as an answer, and seems not inclined to explain why she suddenly would give him his clothing back.

"Right, I guess you need those if you're going to help me…" she snaps coldly. "I guess the pigs will be cold tonight because of you…"

~~~

Now fully dressed - again - in his somewhat musky-smelling clothing, Donta walks across the room and he pulls the small stool from the corner of the room
~~~

and he sits down on the stool rather than on the bed beside the woman. This means he can stare her squarely in the face and prevent her from hiding emotions. He immediately sees that she seems conflicted.

*Hatred. Now sadness. Now a moment of happy memories. Amusement. Sorrow. And now anger once more... What has happened to her before I arrived that has her in this mixed bag of emotions?*

He ties an extra knot in his trousers - from France - that he'd favoured over the breeches worn by most men in Spain still. Compared to the breeches, he could protect himself somewhat better against a renewed assault of interest in his genital. He leaves his shirt open as a distraction that, for all purposes, he was dressed now like he can just leave...

*But should I leave? I vowed to help her...*

"Did you give me back my clothing for me to leave?" he asks, chancing his opportunity to find out if this was really what Carlotta had intended. A head shake answers the question, but then she glances down, almost demurely, like they have caught her out in a lie...

*Is she lying about how she feels about me? Is her behaviour just pretence to get me feel sorry for her? When she doesn't behave in that obnoxious way that she did on the first night, she's actually a friendly person. Is that part of what happens when a person becomes a vampire...?*

# Chapter Ten

Donta feels amazement at his newly discovered ability to determine Carlotta's conflicting emotional state of mind. He studies her face to determine if he can decipher her thoughts, too. But no such luck. It seems she realises how visible her emotions must be to him as she breathes in deeply a few times, looks away, sighs once more, then when she stares back at him her face is as placid as it usually was when he'd probe for information about her past...

It hasn't been the first time that he's seen an emotional woman. He glances down, and for a moment, the memories surface of his mother's behaviour after an evening of his father's drunken stupor when he'd lashed out at his wife for no reason other than her interruption in his ability to settle down with his third bottle of gin.

Donta remembers how he'd usually hide behind the thick curtains of the eastern window of the masia; this reference to homestead isn't one he'd often use as he grew up with being told by his father that they're wealthy - or, at least, should possess it; that they had money - or should be given it; that they have power - or should possess it; that their place within society mattered just as much as that of Quixote of La Mancha.

Yet, unlike his increasingly more famous second cousin, his family never got invited to the court of King Philip IV. His cousin would get invited to the king's court to share accounts of his many adventures. Donta's family, the impoverished part of the same extended family, would never get to visit and only ever see the king from afar.

These were some of the reasons *why* he wants to find his own fortune and fame, and thus, by his *own* effort, to get known by the king, and secure an invitation to the court…

"Carlotta, you *need* to tell me your plan," Donta says. "If your plan fits in with what my plans were, I'll figure out how to get us both in a better place…"

"What do you mean?" Carlotta asks.

"I want to help you," he says tersely. "Let me explain what my plans were… Then you decide whether I can continue on and fulfil my plans or that I'm going to be only here to be as a purpose for yours…"

Carlotta stares wide-eyed at the man for a minute then

grins maliciously before she blurts out, "But you don't even know what the quest is. That makes you such a stupid man for agreeing to something without knowing what it…"

"If we're going to mark people by levels of stupidity, it seems you're as stupid," Donta counters.

"How dare you say that…"

"I dare to say that because of your behaviour," Donta snaps. "I KNOW there's more going on than you want to tell me. If—"

Donta stops speaking abruptly. He stares angrily and annoyed at the woman who has collapsed back onto the bed laughing loudly…

~~~

After ten minutes of him contemplating over her 'quest' he simply nods, and now feeling moody because of its nature, and because of the feeling of foreboding rising in him, he fights the urge to walk from the room. Even with her rather odd hold over him, so perfectly showed in every action over the last fifteen days, he seems to feel the urge to walk off.

And yes, it would require him to walk away from this inn naked, as it will not be likely she'd return his clothes other than forcing him going with her. *But where are we going?* he thinks. *Where's the meeting? Who'll be there? Why do I feel like she's deceiving me when she talks of her cause, her quest, her*
~~~

*mission…?*

"Let's go…" Carlotta quips, curling up her lips playfully.

Donta simply nods as response; he holds his tongue because as he doesn't want to go with her any more. He doesn't want to go to wherever she's going for the quest…

*NOT ANY MORE…*

~~~

Donta angrily stares at Carlotta, feeling dismayed at her actions and her more recent behaviour. She'd indicated to him that she's in danger, but her latest actions had shown *he* was the one in danger, and *not* she. He hadn't understood her intentions - until now - of what she'd meant by her words of him being a companion for *her* cause. The thought of not wanting to go with her keeps persisting in his mind as his stare

Not that she'd explained much about *her* 'cause'…

"Carlotta, what are you doing?" Donta asks in desperation as he tries to pull his hand away, out of the grip she's asserting now. She stares at him coldly, smiling maliciously.

"You don't trick someone you claim to love…" he blurts out, unsure if his words will even have any effect on
~~~

her. "Let me go…"

She stares venomously at him and refuses to explain her actions nor does she loosen her grip on his arm. It reminds Donta of the times when he'd been in a similar iron grip enforced by an irate father on a small boy whenever he'd been in one of his unruly moods and had rampaged through his home without any regard for the others living there. It had been one such day when he'd bumped into his oldest sister and caused her to end up in a chair that was wheeled around for more than a year…

"It seems you're not telling me everything about yourself either, Donta Naughty," she hisses. "I can tell something has you vexed whenever I do this…"

The grip tightens and Donta cringes from the pain she causes with it.

"Alright, I'll go with you but only for this quest of yours…" he hisses.

Only a moment later, he realises he doesn't have the desired effect on Carlotta with his words. Her grip loosens only briefly, and as he watches her face and sees her malicious smile reappear it sees she's back to playing her evil game with him. Her grip tightens even harder now which shows how strong a creature of the night is. The latter had always only been part of a story he'd heard told by the padre, but now it's very real to him. And so is the mortal danger he's now in…

## Chapter Eleven

Donta flinches, but keeps his face neutral. He nods once in reaction to her hard stare at him.

"Let's go…" she hisses, now sounding a lot more menacing. "If you dare to disobey me, I'll make certain you regret you ever left your home…"

~~~

Donta lets Carlotta drag him from the tavern, ignoring the annoyed stare from her father in doing so, especially as the man seemed ready to charge after them yet something was causing him to be stuck in one spot once more. They walk briskly for an hour until they reach a small clearing
~~~

with a narrow stream of water and shade that feels inviting in the squelching heat of the day. The scenery didn't convey the right setting for a resolution of the conflict he had to resolve or the fact that he had to confront her…

"You tricked me into coming here with you," Donta hisses. "But mark my words. This trickery will NOT end well for you…"

Carlotta frowns angrily for a moment, but it's quickly replaced with confusion. Genuine confusion, because, up to now, she'd persuaded Donta to go along with her plans so brilliantly, and had so excellently exerted a similar power over him as she'd done with her own father and with all the men in the tavern.

"But…" she protests. All the previous swagger and superiority has evaporated from her after discovering he has found her out.

"NO! You're a bitch for getting me in this situation," Donta screams. "Do you even think that I can love a BITCH such as you? You're a whore. A nobody. A forsaken nobody. And YOU want ME to love you. I have better choices with my father's cook's daughter, or even the daughter of the poorest man of all this land. A thousand time NO, NO, NO…!"

Donta turns and stomps off.

In the confusion of his outburst, she'd loosened her grip; something he didn't notice himself until he's hundreds of yards away from her. As she stares after him, despair sets in for Carlotta. She glances around, and now for her, the lonely feeling of rejection creeps into her mind.

"What does he mean by it *not* ending well for me?" she whispers. "How? In what way…? In what way will it happen…?"

For the first time in her hundred-year existence as an undead creature of the night, Carlotta feels the wave of mortality pass through her mind. It hits her so hard that she jerks back; like she'd just been struck in the belly by a heavy blunt weapon. Perhaps with a peasant flail that one of the nearby peasants lifted against the creature of the night he'd spotted in the landscape near his abode…

Carlotta turns around feeling deep confusion. She's alone. Well, except for the fast disappearing figure of Donta in the distance, stomping off like he's chased by the devil himself. Now Carlotta realises that in his mind SHE is the devil.

She stumbles backwards, and she sits unexpectedly on a boulder. Her shoulders slump. She feels defeated by an enemy of her own making.

She sighs…

~~~
~~~

## Donta Naughty

Donta stops walking and flops down on a nearby wall. He copies most of Carlotta's actions without realising it. He sighs several times.

"I didn't mean to become so angry with her," he mumbles. "She's a pleasant person when she wants to be… wants to be? Hmm, she wanted me to become like her. Maybe she's lonely like I am…"

For a moment he gets up, but immediately he sits, and he contemplates over the events of the last few days. They'd passed by with the speed of a dust devil like he saw from time to time on the barren fields of more impoverished farmers he'd passed during his travel towards the tavern where he met Carlotta…

"… and I fell in love with Carlotta despite the behaviour shown towards me," he mutters. "Do I really love her…? I have to guess that is a *yes*…"

He gets up and sits again; now feeling indecisive.

After a few minutes, he gets up, after thinking over one of his famous cousin's last adventures; an adventure his cousin would only ever told his family rather telling it in the festivals. Whenever he'd talked about *this* adventure, Dulcinea's face would cloud over, and it was the only time ever she'd looked angrily towards Quixote. It's the only time when the true nature of her origins was put out in the open. And Dulcinea hadn't liked it…

# Donta Naughty

"How will Carlotta react if I offered myself freely and openly for her plan?" Donta whispers, though there is no one to hear his words. "Instead of her forcing me to take part, I offer myself willingly… Can it still make her plan work? It's not a wild party we're going to visit, but if I understand from the few clues told, it's a leadership contest. I can understand her reason if she, a woman, is the only one competing for the leadership of… all the vampires? She's a vampire, and that doesn't seem to bother me…"

Donta frowns, another sigh, and finally he gets up, letting out a momentary groan from painful bones caused by the stone wall, and he slowly starts walking—towards where he'd seen Carlotta last, and he hopes that she's still there.

"What difference will offering my blood willingly will make…?" Donta mutters. "If I do this of my free will, it may be the stories told by the people of my local village will be right or wrong. Now I hope they're going to be *right*—because I might save her from her state of being an undead being…"

Donta's step hastens. A few minutes later, he's running. Another minute later, he's racing at the top of his capacity. He feels surprise when he notices how far he'd walked from her.

He stops a moment to determine his surroundings. In the distance, to his left, he sees the tavern, but its door is closed. If Carlotta had gone back to the tavern, she'd have opened it up for the few patrons that will use it this early in the afternoon.

He glances around, feeling a moment of panic.

He smiles when he spots a familiar figure under a nearby olive tree…

# Chapter Twelve

Donta rushes towards Carlotta and skids to a halt and stands in one spot, panting loudly for a few minutes. Carlotta stares up at him and she looks visibly shocked. She quickly wipes away the tears streaking her face, and after a few breaths, she sets her face to a familiar smirk. Donta ignores all of it…

"Give me your dagger…" he hisses.

"Huh? What?" Carlotta shrieks, and after a minute she hands him her dagger hesitantly.

"Where's the cup?" he hisses.

"Errr… it's in my bag."

"Get it out, and put it here…" he says, pointing at the boulder in front of her.

After a hesitant pause, she complies.

# Donta Naughty

Donta takes a firm grip of the dagger, before he looks at Carlotta for a moment - she stares back at him with worried eyes - he looks at the dagger in his hand again, and in a quick motion he has cut a deep wound in the palm of his other hand, and even though he grimaces for a moment, he squeezes his hand tight and a thick trickle of bright red blood trickles into the cup below.

"Now you have the blood needed for the ritual in there…" Donta says gently; his voice sounding more like he's speaking to a small child. He nods sideways towards where he knows their destination would have been. He sees Carlotta glance quickly in the same direction, before she glances down at the cup.

For a moment her hand moves towards the cup, but just inches from its rim her motions stop, and after a minute she pulls her hand back.

"It's alright," Donta says gently. "I want you to take my blood. I give it willingly…"
She shakes her head.
"You would make an excellent leader for them…" Donta says encouragingly.
Another head shake.
"Why not?" he asks.
"I deceived you…" she whispers. "All I wanted is someone to love me. I deceived you with my actions, words, behaviour…"
Donta kneels in front of Carlotta. With his unblemished hand, he takes hold of Carlotta's chin

tenderly. When their gaze at one another locks, he smiles at her. Her face goes from the fear that has settled on it to a frown to genuine surprise.

"You may have done what you *did* for nefarious reasons but I can see something in your eyes…" Donta says gently. "I'm right in my thinking that you're as lonely as I am—Right?"

She nods.

"Despite the way you behaved, you *did* something right," he continues. "I know we've only known one another a few weeks, and most of it was spent in rambunctious activity but—" He stops speaking for a moment.

"But…?" she asks softly.

"… but despite everything that's happened between us, my heart felt a loss the further I walked from you," he continues gently. "I felt something here."

Donta presses his good hand over his heart. Carlotta's gaze lowers to his chest and holds steady, while he realises she's making specific decisions.

Profound decisions that will affect them both in the end…

~~~

Donta and Carlotta sit side by side until nightfall, which is when it's time to escort her 'companion' to the encampment where over two-hundred other her kind are
~~~

gathering according to her explanations that she speaks in hushed tones.

Before they leave, Donta uses a nearby pond as a mirror and he punctures his neck in two places with the tip of his knife to make it appear that Carlotta had, in fact, sired him. To arrive without this happening to him would spell disaster, as the smell of innocence could cause two-hundred to beset him. She stares at his neck with clear dismay.

"I didn't want *that*," she says.
"I know," he says.
"I don't want *any* of this anymore," she says.
"I know…," he says.

Donta nods at the cup filled with thick red liquid and coaxes her for a while. In the end, she dips a finger in the partly caked blood on his hand and smears it over her teeth, but does so with a horrified grimace over her face.

"It's alright…" he says once more. She nods and wipes away an involuntary tear.

Donta leans forward and kisses her lips; today is the first time she lets him take the lead in any actions of love. After he stops kissing, she leans her head against his chest and listens to the fading heartbeat. They sired him. But not in how the nature of being a vampire dictated. He had given up blood willingly, and this had altered things between them. Neither knew yet in what way or what the coming night would bring…

"We must *go* now…" she whispers, and she pushes Donta away from herself. After a few breaths, she straightens up and from somewhere deep down in her mind she finds the ability to make her voice sound as cold as on the first evening of the meeting, "Come…"

Donta silently nods. He knows now that he needs to comply; to appear to be a sired person who's being led to an unknown fate against his will. He fights off the feeling of fear that enters his mind. He knows he's safe with her, but he knows nothing about the others who will be there.

He glances sideways as they pass the wall once more. Flies gather at the rim of the cup that she never touched. They drink the blood she never wanted to drink. Donta frowns about the cup's purpose. She'd said it was one of the most sacred relics in the possession of someone like her. It was the most sacred relic to be possessed by a vampire.

Yet, she discarded hers when a different vessel filled itself.

Her heart that had been empty for a hundred years now feels the warmth of love for him…

"I love you, Donta…" she whispers, and Donta's gaze goes from the cup to her. She'd stopped walking, and he almost bumps into her.

"I lo—" He wants to say something to her to cheer

her up, but her hands over his mouth to stop him from speaking further.

"I don't want you to say these words until I know how this night treats us…" she whispers. "If I'm a pile of dust tomorrow, you need to say the words to someone… to someone like… errr… like Dulcinea, like your cousin's love… Will you *do* that for me?"

# Chapter Thirteen

Donta frowns momentarily before nodding, and he doesn't realise *yet* that a long-forgotten story from his village will become true by acquiescing to Carlotta's somewhat unusual and annoying demand.

He doesn't know the story will *first* include a long and scary night ends for them both. He just hopes for the best and that the following day he can simply resume his original plans that he'd revealed only partially to the woman beside him.

He flicks glances at her with the frequency and urgency of one who doesn't want to be noticed in their action towards another person. She's staring ahead, unaware of the change of mood in the man beside her.

# Donta Naughty

It filled his gaze with concern, and the burden of feelings he cannot yet share fully with her. He'd said he loves her. He had that as much…

*But did I mean it?*

~~~

Donta glances around at the small clearing they'd arrived at after another half day of walking. He feels hot and there's now an annoying prickle on his neck where two fresh puncture marks are attracting the attention of flies and other annoying insects. The sweat trickling down the side of his neck stings the wounds every time a drop of it brushes over it in slow motion. He feels a temptation to reach up and scratch his neck—and do this with all his nails.

But the first time he reached up to scratch his neck, Carlotta forcefully grabbed his hand and simply shook her head. There could be no sign that he still possesses his own will and was not a loyal creature of the night.

"We need to be careful," she whispers. "If they discover, it will doom us both. I need to appear to be vying for a place on the council. It requires me to… errr… sire you…"

Carlotta seems uncommonly shy suddenly, and Donta reaches for her hand and he squeezes it encouragingly and softly says, "I know what you required to do for this
~~~

meeting. I'm here because I want to help you…"

She nods and visibly swallows hard to kerb the sorrowful emotions she'd been plagued with since mid-afternoon.

"We'll sort this out, and whatever the outcome, remember that you have no fault in this," Donta continues. "You never told me who got you in this situation, or how it happened, but I can see in your eyes how painful that part of your existence was. No, don't explain it to me… It's maybe best I never know if the outcome is not as we want it to be…"

Donta places his forefinger gently over her mouth until he feels her nod, then he removes his finger and glances around to check whether anyone might have seen it. He feels a burden fall away from his mind and heart when it's clear that - so far - they're alone. He almost jumps when Carlotta hisses a few words in a tone as harsh as the day he'd met her.

"I can hear a few of them arriving. They're arriving from the east…"

~~~

From Carlotta's words it becomes clear that she has an advantage over him in terms of being alerted to potential danger. Donta curses inwardly and he knows that had he spoken just a few decibels louder that the newcomers might have heard every word he just spoke to Carlotta, and thus, by his own stupidity would have revealed to every
~~~

other creature of the night - or, as the padre of his church had often enough called them, vampires - that he isn't one of them. It's unclear in what way the lack of his change to one of them would endanger Carlotta. But he sense her fear for this unknown is real.

A single glance at the woman gives him all the telltale signs this is a woman under duress from fear; her lips are quivering; she bits her lips at intervals; her eyes dart to all directions; she plucks at the fringe of her bodice. Her nervousness is rising and it's unsettling to him to see her confidence all but evaporated when it mattered most. But now there were a few dozen people nearby and he couldn't do anything to encourage her, or to be able to still her mind.

Donta takes a chance. He glances around quickly, then concentrates on determining the direction of the wind. It blows towards them; away from the others standing in the clearing. From long forgotten lessons with his father he realises that it means that the creatures of the night are similar to lynxes he had hunted alongside his father who always warned: "If the wind blows in their direction they can smell and hear us."

*I guess I can equate a creature of the night to a predator in that respect*, he thinks.

"Carlotta, listen to me. When the wind blows towards us we can talk…" he hisses under breath and he knows she would hear his words. *But will she understand them as she's no hunter?*

# Donta Naughty

"What do you mean?" she hisses back.

The wind changes direction and she has to wait for an answer and a few minutes later she gets an answer, "Animals smell and hear when the wind blows towards them…"

Her face lights up a moment later when she realises what Donta is implying. Whenever the wind was blowing towards the others around them they can talk. Softly. In short sentences. Perhaps in whispers alone. But it means that she can prepare him fully for what will be happening soon.

So, over the next half an hour she talks, only three or four words at a time, and in a monotone narration that otherwise might have sounded dull to Donta that's becoming increasingly harrowing in nature. It gives clues to the nature of *what* a creature of the night is…

"I guess we're cursed to roam this world to the end of time," she whispers coldly then she looks up at Donta and smiles weakly at him. "But I've been thinking about all this stuff. About what you did to your neck. I have plans. Different from before—can I have a promise that you'll trust me from now on until— If you comply then - well, I hope this shows my love for you - by getting you out of this situation alive… But you must comply with everything I'm going to DO without protest…"

# Chapter Fourteen

Donta hastily nods at the suggestion of a 'plan,' and doesn't to ask her what the proposed plan might be. He just hopes now she's doing the 'right thing' in terms of her behaviour towards him. Deep down, he hopes for a better outcome for her—too!

"Stay here, and you must appear to be submissive next to me at all times," Carlotta whispers. "I must speak to the white-haired man over there. He's the leader of... of everything that you see here around us. He's the leader of... the council. If I want to submit to *be* on the council... to *be* a member of the council, he needs to approve the request..."

Donta has a million questions about who, why, what

for, how... but he stays silent, lowers his head, and forces himself to appear as passive as the others around him who are obviously victims to be sacrificed in the horrid manner had Carlotta had described to him in the last few hours. He forces face to stay as passive as possible as a deep anger wells up inside him about the contrast between yesterday and today.

Yesterday he'd been in the throes of passionate lovemaking with Carlotta with no bothersome thoughts plaguing his mind, whereas today - just over a half day later - he found himself in the middle of what might be the most dangerous part of Spain.

*I doubt Quixote ever had to endure anything similar to this,* Donta thinks. *Compared to this, his adventures almost seem laughable, almost like child's play, almost like the antics of a madman...*

From the corner of eyes, Donta scans his surroundings. The landscape near the old dishevelled barn is a deep shaded valley with steep hills surrounding it, so it offered no way to escape his plight. *If* stories about vampires are true he wouldn't even be able to outrun them.

*She has a plan... I hope she has a plan that allows me to be alive tomorrow morning...*

Donta wonders what Carlotta is telling the three vampires she'd approached. *Is she telling them that he isn't one of them? Or is she trying to fool them into thinking she's good enough to be part of their council.*

Her glances towards him don't make him feel confident of the situation across the courtyard in front of the old barn that's menacing in its appearance to his already agitated mind. He stares up at the old building which now almost appears to be like the mouth of one of the gargoyles carved into the stone wall on either side of the entrance of his local church which had always felt like overgrown monsters to him as a child.

*But now I'm surrounded by monsters…how many are there here? How many of them are creatures of the night, are vampires… like Carlotta? She's told me finally she's one of them but…why am I here…?*

~~~

Donta follows Carlotta when she motions him to follow her a few hours later after the small valley  around him has enveloped into the dusk of the approaching evening. He realises that this night is going to the worst night. A wordless prayer, the first ever since learning it as a child, escapes his lips.

"Hush…"

Donta shuts up at the hissed command from the woman beside him. His eyes dart around to determine who
~~~

else may have heard him, remembering how excellent Carlotta's hearing is.

"It's okay. Please continue praying," she says a moment later. "I might need a prayer too. He doesn't quite trust me…"

The 'he' would be the man that Carlotta had been speaking to earlier in the evening. Donta frowns and casts a quick glance toward the man who stands on a small platform at the darkest part of the barn. A man, deceptively appearing to be in his mid-sixties, stands staring at the large crowd packing themselves into the barn. All walking to a bale of hay, a wooden bench or a clear spot on the floor. Donta feels his fear grow when he catches the gaze of this man, obviously the leader, and although Carlotta's demanding yank to get him to sit on the floor is assured in its outward appearance, it's her eyes that betray her own fear.

Donta blinks twice. She nods gently. It's their signal to communicate assurance.

"We need to be careful," she whispers. "He has accepted my pledge to join the council but he claims he senses something different about you compared to all others."

Donta blinks twice again, then he glances down before he whispers softly, "I'm afraid but let everything happen as it should do for this event…"

# Donta Naughty

"I can't promise safety for you until the sun rises once more," she says.

"I realise that," Donta replies. "But it feels to me that somehow you were duped too. If we both survive this, promise me to tell me how... how this... happened to you, alright?"

"I will tell you all about myself if we survive this," Carlotta whispers. "I promise..."

She turns and walks to the other end of the bench where she sits down, obviously sighing deeply.

Donta watches her from the corner of his eye, and feels a deep sorrow rise in his mind. He feels a deep sadness about the possibility that his newly-found love for this mysterious woman would be so short-lived. Either he'd be dead in the morning or she'd be dead.

*It sounds so much like that play that those performers did when father took all of us to the city, he thinks. In that play he had found true love, then she dies and he hears of her death, finds her dead and then kills himself only for her to find him dead beside her. Will it go like that for us? Will I appear dead to her tomorrow for her to walk out into the sun to kill herself only for me to wake up safely...?*

Donta glances sidelong and catches her gaze. It seems she's thinking of a similar situation for him to happen. She mouths a few words before her gaze jerks back towards the darkest part of the building.

# Chapter Fifteen

Donta realises he *cannot* tell Carlotta similar words as she'd spoken, so hastily as any attempt of communicating with Carlotta on his part might get noticed by the man at the front of the building. But her words influence him. They give him courage and a renewed will to live to survive this evening.

He glances at the other 'victims' there. Their faces show they are all feeling a deep fear. Their companions seem to be more inclined to increase their feelings of despair, unlike Carlotta, who just sits passively at the other end of the small bench. Her expression is chiselled in stone. She bites her lips. She crumples the edge of her skirt.

# Donta Naughty

Even his less sensitive nostrils smell the surrounding fear. It's oozing in the surrounding air. He wonders how the sensation is for the woman, and she seems to wrinkle her nose from time to time like she's attempting to ignore what must be overwhelming her…

~~~

Darkness falls speedily over the landscape outside the building and turns the inside of the barn - that's now lit up by a few small torches - into a spectacle of grotesque shadows and shapes that might have escaped from hell itself. Or from some nightmarish world. Or a nightmare…

*This all feels like a god-forsaken nightmare*, Donta thinks. *Why did I ever end up here? Why did I leave my home in the first place?*

Now he realises he knows the answer to a question that has plagued him for the last three weeks. He's facing punishment for his unruly behaviour *before* leaving home. Like others around him Donta has as much fear for the punishment from God, though he'd always convinced himself he wouldn't let it guide his life. Now when it matters most his mind can do nothing else than pray for mercy from that *same* God for the end, if it came soon, to be swift and decisive.

The stories told by the simple folk from neighbouring villages close to Donta's house was of the doom that
~~~

would befall any such person who turns away from God; they would tell that such a person would be struck down by God's wrath when morning comes…

Donta glances at the man at the back of the barn who seems to tower over the spectacle going on in front of him and who seems unmoved by the plight the many victims dropping to the floor one by one. There was no need for Donta to put the visualisation of each person's end into his mind any more. Definitely not after he sees this dark, mysterious man pull a woman of a similar age to Carlotta towards him. When the woman drops dead the gushing blood makes Donta recoil with disgust.

*Almost like they're cattle being butchered,* Donta thinks as he remember witnessing the butcher slaughtering a lamb in the side room of the stables at home; it had been his first witnessing of such bloodletting. But it had prepared him for when his father took him to see the bull fights in Madrid. It was a month away from home and he hadn't enjoyed a single day of the events. On arriving home he'd sought comfort in his mother's arms and cried on her shoulders. *Something about me going to Mother to get comforted had caused Father to start drinking more and be so abusive to Mother…*

Donta knows he cannot blame himself for the behaviours between his parents. The padre at the local church, who also told the stories about the creatures of the night, had said so. The small boy found between the pews was remorseful beyond reason yet became a rebellious sullen person just a few years later. It was this later behaviour that had caused him to be here, in this barn, right now and in a staring match with one of the most vile creatures he'd ever met.

*Not even wolves or other predators out there in the wilderness are like this towards their prey,* Donta thinks with disgust wrinkling his nose as the man plainly wipes his mouth with the sleeve of his tunic and thus smearing the blood over his stubble of face. Then he sneers at Donta…

Donta jerks his gaze away from the man. Carlotta, who sits close, pulls him back in a similar motion Donta saw happen to the woman at the man's feet only a few minutes earlier.

"Play along," she hisses in his ear. "When I pull away you slump back and don't move a muscle…"

Donta blinks once to indicate he understands; they'd agreed on this signal if at any time he couldn't speak.

Carlotta takes on an animalistic appearance in the next moment. She grunts loudly. Her face is so close to Donta's face and neck that he feels her hot breath. Their eyes lock and she stares back with growing fear.

"This wasn't what I wanted…" she whispers.

"I know…" he whispers back.

They both cast their gaze towards the others present. The sounds of others there being used for the purpose of allowing the creatures of the night there - the vampires similarly to Carlotta - to compete for a place on the coveted 'council' that was promised to them by the mysterious dark figure overlooking everything from the darkness of the deepest part of the barn.

"I don't want this…" Carlotta says resolutely. "Not any more. I don't care if he punishes me tomorrow…"

"I'll play along until we know it's safe," Donta whispers. "I'm here because I love *you*…"

"How can you love me after everything I did?" she counters.

"Have you always been this way…? With your attitude towards others…?" he asks. "I'm asking because I'm certain you're a much nicer person than you make it out to me…"

"I guess I changed my behaviour to fit in with what *he* wants…" Carlotta whispers, now nodding sidelong towards the mysterious man; more openly than Donta expected her to do.

Then her face is against his neck and even though she doesn't bit it feels to him she could do this any moment…

**Donta Naughty**

**Chapter Sixteen**

Donta recoils when the people near him pull a woman closer, and in a fast motion he has his teeth sunk deep in her neck. She looks surprised by the motion, then it's replaced by a horrified appearance and then her face goes passive before she slumps to the ground.

*It's what Carlotta wanted to do to me initially,* he thinks. *But... why didn't she in the end? Does she really love me, like she said to me...?*

One by one, a creature of the night moves towards an intended victim before copying the actions of the *first* person to do this. They all sink their teeth into the necks of the victims.

# Donta Naughty

Donta glances at Carlotta and sees her recoil in equal measure. Now that she's being shown visually what she'd intended to do to the man beside her, it disgusts her.

*She refused to go ahead with it,* he thinks. *What changed for her?*

Donta glances sidelong at the woman beside him. Their eyes meet once again. There is fear in her eyes now, and occasionally darts her gaze from person to person around them. The others around them are slowly becoming more and more overtaken by their bestial need of devouring the blood of their victims. Donta sees a flash of a familiar knife similar to the one that Carlotta had brandished and that he'd used to puncture his own neck.

But the knife is wielded by the creatures of the night who give their victims no choice...

*She left hers behind,* he thinks. *The leader may notice it...*

Donta looks from the corner of his eye towards the towering figure standing in the darkness of the deepest part of the building. The darkness makes the man a lot more menacing than before; more menacing than when everyone had just been busying themselves with their own things.

Now, the tide has turned and things are taking on an increasingly menacing feeling to it.

# Donta Naughty

Donta feels his heart beating faster and feels the prickle of sweat pearls on the back of his neck. The feeling of fleeting safety is evaporating faster than the sweat pearls on his neck. He feels a presence near him and looks sideways to find Carlotta close by him. "We need to pretend to be doing similar," she hisses under her breath. "Or *he* may notice we didn't do the ritual..."

"You mean the cup and knife that you left behind near the tree...?"

She nods curtly.

~~~

Donta realises that the first hour of the activities is only the beginning of a night of terror now. Both for himself and for the woman beside him. The fleeting moments of them expressing their love towards one another becomes a game. He attempts multiple times to reassure Carlotta, and also constantly has to fight off showing his true feelings for her every time she smiles back at him and then whispers, "I love you as well..."

*It feels like one of those plays that was occasionally performed by the visiting performers*, Donta thinks. *Such as one that always shows the lovers with a happy ending. Will we have a happy ending too...?*

"Carlotta, when this stuff is over, will we be able to
~~~

leave? In the plays I saw as a child, it often enough happened in that way…" he asks gently under his breath.

Donta knows he risks much by speaking now, and by speaking in a louder, more confident voice.

"Shush…"

"I think we need to show *we* are better than him in everything we do," Donta counters. "If *we* work together, he has less power over us. Like it always happens to the bad person in the stories or plays…"

Carlotta stares at the dark figure for a few moments, then she turns back and nods once at his comment.

"Do they come from their plight alive in these stories and plays you grew up with?" she asks flatly.

"Not always, but their souls are often saved…" Donta says, now feeling a need to be honest. "But when they come from the danger alive, they're always able to live their lives in peace and with no one ever impeding their love or happiness…"

She nods.

"I want that for us…" he adds hastily.

Another nod.

"I will honour the promise made about finding someone else if I survive this…" he whisper. "But… but I love you *too* much to really want that."

Carlotta smiles at him warmly. None of her previous pretence of being a spiteful creature is reflected in the smile she shows him.

"I can see your true nature in your smile," he says. "Am I right when I suggest that as a child you were a sensitive person who cared about people?"

She nods once, then says, "I can't talk about it now…"

# Donta Naughty

"I understand it," he continues. "Would you be willing to do so if we're still both alive tomorrow?"

Carlotta looks away and stares ahead pensively for several minutes, then she turns back to him and says, "If I survive this, it's a promise. What I can say now is that certain things happened to me that made me a bitter person..."

Donta decides not to comment, but the comment confirms in part that there was a lot more going on with Carlotta; both in terms of her personal history and her presence in this building.

"You don't need to explain if it endangers you... or us," Donta whispers. "If a time comes that, you can talk about it, then just tell as much as you feel comfortable to talk about. I remember Mother always telling me about her true feelings about how Father was treating her. For now, just remember that I love you with all my soul and heart and that I will do as much as I can do to keep you safe from all of this..."

Donta hears Carlotta snort a giggle for a moment, then she nods at him before she says, "I will do the same and of the two of us I have a lot more capability of—Just know I love you too... very much..."

# Chapter Seventeen

Now the reassurance of each of their feelings is confirmed both their attention turns towards the activities going on around them. Of the two of them, Donta has to be more careful with his general behaviour, and he has to act passively. Calling forth every memory of the plays and stories from his childhood, Donta 'plays along' to appear to now be a creature of the night under *her* full control…

*I'm certain this is going to be a dangerous night for us both. For me, if they discover, it has not made me into one of them. For her, if they discover her deception. I think that man hiding in the shadows there is the most dangerous of them all. He's like one of those wild animals who gets the devil's sickness in their minds that makes them froth. The blood on his mouth can be so similar to that…*

# Donta Naughty

This new thought sets in motion a new perspective for Donta. He nudges Carlotta carefully. She jerks at the sudden contact between them.


"I think I figured it out," he whispers. "He's using some witchcraft for this ritual, too. The bowl and knife were for that…"

"Witchcraft?"

"Yes, and by not using that element of the ritual, we can save ourselves from him," he whispers back. "If I'm right, we just have to survive the next five hours until sunrise…"

Carlotta stares at Donta wide-eyed then realisation sets in for her and she says, "Do you think I'm going to be alright too?"

"Well, to be honest, I cannot be certain," he admits, frowning worriedly, "But… if—well, I better tell you everything I've figured out if we are still here tomorrow. Alive, I mean, by the way. He cannot know about it…"

Donta nods sideways towards the figure in the darkness.

"I think he already suspects something is different about us…"

"I never asked for the carnage that's happening right now," Carlotta whispers. "I don't want to be part of his council if it means going through all this every time…"

"We can go away tomorrow, away from—" he suggests.

"Where can we go?" she interjects.

"Remember my plans…"

She nods.

"I want you to be a part of those plans…" he suggests.

"I have to think about it," she says. "And only give you an answer tomorrow if I'm here still…"

"When you're here still there are more things I can talk with you about," Donta says reassuringly.

Carlotta gazes at him for several minutes then says, "I have to admit that I don't recognise you from that first night. You've changed. You've become a better person. Someone I can love if I keep admitting to more truths…"

"I'm glad you think of me in this way," Donta whispers, looking down. "There are things about me I've never told you. Things that shame me now about my behaviour. Things that made me too similar to my father, and I didn't listen when Mother said this about me. It's why I rebelled… I guess…"

"I think I would shame you if you knew the truth about me," Carlotta whispers. "I can't talk about it…"

"I guessed days ago that something happened to you," Donta says. "Am I right it is something to do with your mother?"

Carlotta nods curtly.

"If we survive this night and I've told you about what we can do next with our lives, then you decide whether you want to tell me," Donta says firmly. "I will respect whichever decision you make. It's proof of my love for you to respect you…"

"It's the first time someone's been as kind towards me as you are now," Carlotta whispers. "Especially after the way I treated you. I was so horrible to you…"

"I saw a kind heart underneath it all," he continues. "When you glanced towards your father on that first night and he had that icy stare—Well, I've seen a similar stare from my father towards my mother. She always said it was his way to make her feel less valuable, less wanted… I knew from that behaviour from your father he was a similar sort of person."

"He never loved Mother," she whispers. "He knows him…"

Carlotta nods towards the dark shape of the burly man standing in the deepest part of the barn.

"Ah… right," Donta exclaims, now realising that some of his own assumptions about the plight of this woman's mother might be even more dire than he first realised.

"Is she…?" he asks but stops remembering her words from moments ago. He realises that even the hint of information she volunteered was probably hard for her to cope with.

"If I'm alive still tomorrow, I'll tell you," she says. "If I'm not, then use it to always seek a way to give justice to any woman in peril you may meet. Promise me that too…"

"I promise," Donta answers with no hesitation. "And you and your mother will be the *first* avenged."

"Thank you…"

They give each other a quick glance, and Donta smiles fleetingly at her.

"Remember that I love you," he whispers, even quieter than before. "Let it give you the strength needed to get through this night. Also, I hope that my prayer from earlier gets answered…"

She smiles broader at the comment, and her eyes light

up with the realisation of what he'd asked for. To get salvation for her, a creature of the night, or as most people might call it, a vampire to get the salvation from the only being capable of true salvation, and in a land governed by faith that meant God, and perhaps even a blessing later from a padre.

"Do you mean we...?" she asks.

After a glance around, Donta places a finger over her lips, then he nods encouragingly at her.

"I think I understand what you're telling me," she says. "I think have more hope now than I had an hour ago when all *this* started. I love you *too*..."

# Donta Naughty

# Chapter Eighteen

The darkness of the night outside suddenly becomes more and more appealing, and Donta and Carlotta glance constantly towards the doorway as each of their desire to leave grows. Their fear is causing them to inch closer and find solace in one another.

A hand reaches for to other person's hand every moment they think it is safe to do this. Each time they think the mysterious man casts a gaze in their direction, they pull their hands back. Slowly it becomes a game...
"He's gone..." Donta hisses suddenly.
"Huh what?"
"He's not there anymore..." Donta says.

Carlotta looks toward where the man had stood so

long that he might even appear like one gargoyle found on the facade of a church. She nods quickly to confirm his findings, then stares puzzled at Donta.

"But… I didn't do the ritual," she says. "How can you have the senses of a vampire like I do?"

"Maybe there's more to the ritual than we realise right now," Donta hisses. "Maybe it binds one's will to his. Look around you. All the others here are acting… odd."

Carlotta glances around then when she looks back at Donta her face has a puzzled expression, like she's trying to solve a mystery of some sort, and she asks, "Do you think he knows?"

Donta shakes his head. He doesn't know. Or more precisely, he wants to believe he knows an answer to *all* the questions she might ask now. He smiles encouragingly at her. She smiles back. In this moment of danger there wasn't much either could do to express in deeper detail the love felt for the other person, however ever small measure of feelings they *could* express to one another was increasing the determination for him or her to survive the night…

"It's only a few more hours to go until morning," Donta whispers. "It is the darkest time of the night outside. It means we have to be alright for another four hours and then—"

"… And then we know whether you have to keep your promises to me *or* whether I'm alive still," Carlotta says coldly. "I'm getting angrier by the minute at both of them for what they did to me…"

Donta frowns a bit at the words, and quickly realises that the anger and coldness present in her words - or her voice - are not directed at him.

"I love you, Donta," she says softly. "I'm not angry with you. Just so you know this. You've given me hope this night. Before this night—before you ever arrived—I only knew that somehow I could take revenge, and the only way was to get on the council. Then after—well, actually I was uncertain what to do next…"

"So the revenge is, and I'm assuming this based on your earlier words, is for something that happened to your mother?" he asks. "If you don't want to tell me, then just don't tell me."

She simply nods an answer. It tells Donta enough to understand, and he's about to speak once more when she hisses with added urgency, "He's—back…"

~~~

"SILENCE…!!!"

Donta and Carlotta jerk, and they move closer to one another, caused by the malice in the man's voice. Donta takes hold of Carlotta's hand, but she pulls it away only a moment later. She gives him an icy stare for a moment, then softens her gaze and shakes her head ever so slightly. Donta looks down.

"Tonight the dawn of a new age begins for our kind…"

Donta frowns angrily at the words. He knows what
~~~

beings are around him. He knows may be one of them. He glances sidelong, then he mutters a brief prayer, "Please, if you *are* merciful, let this night be easy for us both, and let it *end* without either of us feeling pain or suffering…"

He glances again at Carlotta, then hears her next word, "Amen…"

"We will get through whatever is going to happen next…" he hisses.

In the dim light of the few candles, the surrounding people are turning into something as grotesque as the gargoyles adorned on the local church near his home.

"The plans I have for us all will mean that we will command this world…"

"That's not what he had told me before about this council…" Carlotta hisses angrily through her teeth. "He said the goal was for us all to good things and help people. He lied to me…"

"Shh, or he may hear you…"

"I hope he does and hope that God does too, so if he does something bad to me that God is there to punish him for it," Carlotta hisses. "I had enough of being lied to… He lied to me, and so did my father…"

Carlotta looks at Donta and then her expression softens a bit and she adds, "I know you said there were things about yourself that shame you, but you've never lied to me. I know this to be true…"

"I learnt from my mother that lying to someone you genuinely care about and love is never good," Donta whispers. "But despite it happening to her, she stays with him…"

"Your father?"

Donta nods once.

"Is that the reason you left your home?"

Another nod, and he adds, "Mother said to me it's too late for her to do something else with her life. She said for me to find someone to love, come home with her, then ask—no, demand a blessing from Father—and then I should leave and never come back…"

"Oh, right…" Carlotta says softly. "I now understand why you didn't want to speak about your family…"

"But neither do you and you just admitted to—"

"SILENCE! I SAID SILENCE FROM ALL…"

Donta jerks away from Carlotta to the other end of the bench, and her reaction was similar. They glance sheepishly at one another, then each sees in the other's eyes that this night is far from over…

# Chapter Nineteen

The sounds around Donta grow in magnitude as the mysterious man speaks in a booming voice. The longer he speaks, the more menace is present in his words. His behaviour becomes more abrupt and in the end, every voice is chanting a few words in a language that Donta doesn't understand.

"What's he doing?" Donta whispers, hoping that Carlotta will hear him speaking. He glances sidelong towards the woman who shakes her head hastily, then appears to be chiselled in stone.

The man repeats the chant and slowly the voices around Donta become louder, more menacing and take on the sound of animals ravaging their prey. Donta forces his mind to ignore the surrounding sounds. He shuts his eyes for a moment, then breathes deeply before he straightens up and gives pretence to be taking part in the chants himself. But no sound comes from his mouth. He feels his lips moving, but that's about it.

"Pretend to be taking part in this chant…" Donta whispers before he continues his own pretence.

A glance sideways he sees Carlotta behave similarly, even though her face expression and facial colour show that she's not alright with her current actions.

"I love you, Carlotta. Let it give you strength…" he whispers once again when he sees the mysterious man with his back to them. She straightens up in a reaction to his words, blinks twice slowly. She seems to breathe in deeply for a moment then he sees a familiar, somewhat malicious smile settle around her lips. But her gaze is settled towards the mysterious man.

Slowly, Donta's ears notice something odd about Carlotta's way of chanting the wording.

*They sound wrong compared to how everyone else is saying them,* he thinks. *I hope he doesn't notice it. Because if he does, she's in danger. This is what she meant earlier about my life possibly being in danger…*

"WE are the new world order…"

# Donta Naughty

Donta fights the urge to laugh at the world thinking, *Yes, and that's also what my father thinks too with him thinking he's better than others...*

As the chant continues, the shape of the mysterious man seems to become larger and more menacing to Donta. He pulls a man closer, then a moment later the man is a lifeless pile at the man's feet. Next it is a woman, then another two men, and another woman.

"MY plan is for everyone to join us. MY plan is for all the world to become like we are..."

Donta frowns for a moment. Now the words cut deep. Everyone could mean that his mother could end up like Carlotta, and he'd already seen how badly it had affected the woman sitting a few yards from him. He glances sidelong towards her, and she seems to stare at the floor now. Her shoulders are shaking somewhat.

*She's weeping over her plight*, Donta thinks. *She understands what has happened to her...*

"No..." Donta blurts out. The moment he'd voiced his opposition, he realises that the danger for himself has suddenly been heightened by one simple word of opposition. He glances up towards the man who had stopped his stride towards the darkest part of the barn. He turns slowly...

Their gazes lock, and it becomes a power play of will.

# Donta Naughty

After a few moments, Donta feels his lips are moving once more. Chanting the unknown words, however, there's no substance to them. The mysterious man turns away and beckons over yet another of the victims towards him. Another dead body drops to the floor a moment later.

Donta glances around, mentally counting the number of people there…

*If I'm right, it's at least a hundred, maybe two hundred here,* Donta thinks. *But I can tell now who of them is a vampire. They all lured the victims here like Carlotta lured me here. But all of them are already turned. I can tell by the caked blood on their necks…*

Donta frowns again and realises that his self-inflicted cuts seem "clean" compared to the way others appear. It's likely the mysterious leader will notice it soon enough.

*What will happen to Carlotta if he discovers I'm not a true creature of the night?* Donta thinks, and he feels worry rising in his mind now. *She could be in danger already…*

"ALL RISE…"

The pull of the words is irresistible in Donta's mind. He gets on his feet. It feels now like the end could come soon. The end would be a release from the nightmare he finds himself in now. A nightmare that would slowly unfold and last at least another three hours…

~~~
~~~

# Donta Naughty

The last moments of horror come for Donta soon enough when he sees the mysterious man now beckoning Carlotta, of all people, over to himself. She seems to become mesmerised by the man by an unknown method of control. She walks towards him and stands there dazed, like she's unaware of her surroundings.

"Don't let him get to you," Donta whispers. "Resist him…"

Donta wills with his own mind for Carlotta to turn her head towards him. It seems to happen and a moment later, their eyes lock. It breaks the spell over her and she rushes back to the bench, where she curls up into a tight ball. She's shaking with fear now.
The mysterious man laughs loudly at the reaction he had caused to them both, then nonchalantly continues his bloody ritual of picking off victims as a sacrifice.

"Are you alright?" Donta whispers. She nods once.
"Just keep pretending it scares you," Donta continues. "If we survive this carnage for the next two hours, then we'll be alright. It will be morning soon enough…"

He hopes there is a measure of truth in his words because now the first ones to have turned into true creatures of the night are getting up from the floor and moving towards the benches near the walls. A room filled with predators, with themselves being the prey…

# Donta Naughty


# Chapter Twenty


Donta opens his eyes slowly, and he glances around cautiously. First, he's certain the night had, in fact, turned *him* also into a creature of the night. Though he'd been made into one by his actions of offering himself up the previous day. However, he immediately knows that something is like how he had felt the previous afternoon, just after he had punctured his own neck with Carlotta's dagger as a demonstration of his love towards her. He reaches up and feels the surface of his neck.

*There are two scabs present on his neck… only, and they're both healing up,* he thinks. *This means that she never bit my neck as I saw others do last night. It means she omitted part of the actions the leader demanded from them all…*

# Donta Naughty

He glances towards the location where Carlotta had been sitting. She's sprawled out on the low bench and seems asleep. He feels a momentary relief. She seems to be safe. For now. And she seems to sleep peacefully. For now.

Donta feels a wave of warmth pass through him as he watches her. The same feeling as the previous day when he confessed to himself how he felt about the woman. His gaze becomes a hard gaze, willing for the woman to wake up. But nothing happens, and she continues sleeping.

After a few minutes, Donta senses something else. He glances around to be met by the direct gaze of the old man, who'd been showed to him to be the council's leader. Their eyes meet, and for several moments Donta feels the same uncanny pull that he'd felt whenever Carlotta had stared at him. He tears his eyes away, blinks a few times to settle his mind, then wills himself to stare once more at the man. But the pull on his mind is gone now. All he sees now is a strange man who seems to grow disturbed.

*Something is happening…*

~~~

A final angry, but equally worried, gaze - the ultimate moment of worry before everything changes for Donta - comes from the leader who is sitting upright on a hay bale in the darkest part of the barn.
~~~

# Donta Naughty

Donta never knew the man's name, where he'd come from, but as he watches the man slowly turn from a being of flesh and bones to dust, it proves this man isn't from the local region. He studies the man and realises this man might have come from somewhere in the eastern parts of Europe. He'd brought the dangerous world of being a creature of the night with him, and as the two men stare at one another, Donta realises that he, a sullen young man who was clueless about the world around him, and who'd always been a rebel, had rid the world of the danger this man represents.

The man turns to dust…

Then, a moment later, the same happens to a woman beside him…

~~~

Donta gapes as one by one the creatures of the night, around him, silently turn to small piles of white dust. Now, the words from their 'new' leadership from an eternity as a vampire are just empty words and what's happening right now is proving this to be happening. Their eternity has come but, in Donta's mind, the answer comes as clear as the sunlight filling the barn, *I guess the padre was right about vampires all along*, Donta thinks, as he feels some relief for even surviving one of the most dangerous nights in his entire life.
~~~

# Donta Naughty

*I guess their immortality is doomed and punishment in hell…*

Darting his gaze towards Carlotta, Donta stares at the woman and he almost expects to see the same to happen to *her* at any moment. But she's bathed in the specks of sunlight streaming through the small imperfections of the wooden frame of the building.

He smiles when his mind compares her posture in her slumber to an innocent child and realises she's curled up similarly to a child on the bench beside him. He waits a few minutes more, then when nothing isn't happening he sighs relief.

*She hasn't jumped up screaming from pain from the sunlight covering her…*

He glances down when he feels a warmth on his own hands, and that he realises he, too, is bathed in sunlight.

*Something is definitely different for us compared to all the others,* he thinks, glancing around, and now he sees the hundreds of small piles of white dust scattered on every surface around him.

A brush of wind, and they're all gone…

"Carlotta, please wake up—" he whispers, and despite speaking softly, his voice echoes in the empty building.

# Donta Naughty

She opens her eyes slowly and stares up at him for a few minutes. After a few minutes, she notices their surroundings. She glances around and back at Donta. "Where's everyone?"

"Gone…" he answers plainly.

"Gone where? There are things supposedly done after—" she shrieks.

"*Not* where, just *gone*…" Donta interjects, and he points at one of the few remaining white dust piles on an opposite bench. She glances towards it, and screams out loud when it gets carried away by the wind. She clasps her mouth and stares wide-eyed at him, then somehow finds her normal voice again, asking, "Was *that* one of them?"

A plain, somewhat abrupt nod is all she gets from the man beside her, because he doesn't really know how he can answer any of her questions adequately.

Her face blanches. Her body slumps. Tears stream down her face.

He doesn't need to answer her possible next question, or after that, when a gust of wind blows the barn door wide open and bathes the entire building, and them too, in the scorch of sunlight.

The answer of what has happened to them, and to all the others, around them, is delivered to them both by the grace of a higher being whose mercy now manifests itself to them…

# Donta Naughty

# Chapter Twenty-One

Donta gently takes hold of Carlotta's hand. He knows of the local stories told about vampires in the region where he lives. How they'd end up turning into dust in the sun; and thus, forever, would be liberated from this curse. But there's another small part of the story that is *rarely* told. The part of *true* love found in rare cases between the cursed creatures of the night…

In an odd sort of way, Donta realises he may have got the *same* thing as his more famous cousin. But for entirely different reasons and differently that no one from his family would ever believe.

He glances sidelong at Carlotta, who'd started out as a different sort of person. She'd been manipulative. She'd been deceptive. Yes, even vile in his mind. But now, he sees someone who he wants to genuinely love. And to love with all his being, heart and soul. If he even had a soul after being sired by her… but he realises she never sired him in the way it's always told in the local stories.

"I love you, Carlotta…"

She shows relief on her face at hearing the words. The tenseness leaves her body. She becomes relaxed. She seems to accept fate may not be kind to them in the next few minutes. Or, at least, that's how he interprets her mouth motions, seemingly willing the sun to comply with the four words he'd just said to her with a loud voice that echoed in the surrounding landscape.

"Whatever happens next, I genuinely LOVE you…" he bellows. She glances at him, and he smiles warmly at her.

*My smile has more heat than the sun if I interpret the worry knot on her forehead correctly.*

A moment later, they are both staring ahead again as the dusky blue of night becomes a shade of blood red; it becomes a dark orange, followed by a bright sunflower yellow matching the flowers in the field beside them. As the sky above them becomes azure blue, they stare amazed at the sun; both of them are squinting at the yellow ball rising above the distant mountain range.

"How is this possible?" Carlotta whispers, "How?"

"I think—" Donta says, but he immediately pauses before adding, "We've conquered *true* love and did it against all odds, and we've shown the world that we can love *too*…"

"You're right, but I also think that we broke something when I refused to…" she says.

"It's in the past now," Donta says as he reaches sideways and kisses her on her forehead. "In the end, you showed you loved me for genuine reasons, and that won my heart over…"

"Can you forgive me?"

"I showed you I forgave because I agreed to come here…" he answers, "Actions often show so much more than words alone."

They stare again at the sun that's now higher in the sky, and that's casting warmth over the landscape. They hold up their hands in the sunlight, holding them closely side by side. They stare, fascinated, as nothing happens. Nothing of what they saw happen to others the previous morning seems to happen to either of them. The others, who'd been at the gathering with them and who'd vied for leadership, had not been so fortunate. Neither had their chosen victim been fortunate.

From behind a curtain, but in different rooms, Donta and Carlotta had watched as one after another, the vampires all had turned into piles of dust. None of them had survived daytime. Now their time had come and things were so massively different that it shocks him, and perhaps also shames him, about each of their behaviours…

"Maybe… do you believe we *can* go into a church for a blessing?" she asks. "If we enter, and nothing happens…"

"I guess that's our next test," he answers.

"Do you know any near here?" she asks.

"We can go towards my home. I passed a church soon after I left my home…" he suggests.

"Yes… please," she says plainly.

They walk, now acutely aware of their surroundings. In the nearby farming fields, they see women and children walk towards the crops waiting for harvesting. Unlike three days earlier, the morning after the gathering, Donta feels no urges or the pain numbing hunger. Something is different today.

*What is so different? Is it because I forgave her?* Donta thinks, *It could be. I remember the store of Don Quixote. Is Carlotta my Dulcinea?*

Donta looks sidelong at the woman beside him who'd started off as a wild, disobedient daughter, who'd wanted him to be like her. She'd used her sadistic charm to great effect by even putting her *own* father under her spell.

*The owner of the tavern now behaves like he doesn't remember the last decade or so. Perhaps for the best, too…*

Donta remembers the story the padre lik of the local church near his house had told. The story had mostly been a warning for the congregation to be cautious of the creatures that would lure you to doom. He contemplates how the padre will react if he was told who or what Carlotta and he are. Would he splash them over with holy water? Would he banish them from the church? Would it amaze him to hear about them walking in broad daylight from the tavern to his church? Donta doesn't know, but he wants to discover.

The story the padre had told to the villagers and the Don - Donta's stern father - and his family including an unruly boy called Donta, the blessing from a padre *would* remove all the traces of the curse that make a person a creature of the night, "If creatures of the night walk in daylight unharmed, and they enter a church such as this one, and they've only ever lusted for *true* love, and *not* for the impurities of drinking each other's blood…" he had said.

Somehow, the recent events have triggered Donta to remember the tale ever so vividly…

# Donta Naughty

# Chapter Twenty-Two

As Donta takes hold firmly of Carlotta's hand with his unblemished hand, a momentary thought enters his mind, *She didn't want to taste my blood, in the end. In the end, I sliced into my hand and put some blood into a cup...*

Donta glances sidelong, and a new thought enters his mind, *Was it me sacrificing willingly that made it different for us? In the end, she chose pure love over the leadership in their council, and because of this decision, she was rejected by them. She had tricked me into giving up my blood, but when she refused first my blood and she showed genuine remorse... I forgave her because of those choices...*

He hides the frown from the woman beside him by looking away for a few minutes.

# Donta Naughty

They walk in a northerly direction…

As the morning turns to a sunny, sultry afternoon and Donta and Carlotta arrive at the top of a hill, they stop, and she stares amazed at the bright green of the valley below.

"That's home…" Donta says quietly. He points east of their location towards the massive white building. "It *will* surprise my family that I'm returning with a woman to love, and who is my betrothed. I grew up always hearing about Don Quixote and his Dulcinea so much that it put ideas in my head. But I found a woman to love like he loves her… Even if my circumstances are odd, and *not* the material for stories to tell at fireplaces…"

"I'd rather they don't know about that part about me," Carlotta whispers.

"From this moment no one except for the padre will know this about you," Donta says. "According to the story I heard him tell, we have to confess to him about what has happened between us and to us afterwards. If he's accepting of our forgiveness for one another, he'll bless us, and if we can convince him to wed us, we'll be free of the curse…"

"I hope he's as forgiving as you made him out to be as you told in your story," Carlotta says.

"Shall we go?"

She nods.

They walk back slowly to the small path that's commonly used by goat herders. They'd arrived by a method that leaves them mostly unnoticed by most people; at least, until after they *know* that they're wed by the padre.

If such a thing is even possible for them…

T he sky is filling with the pinks and purples of early evening when Donta and Carlotta arrive at the outskirts of the furthest village. They pause as they walk; always expecting someone to run at them with a pickaxe or hay fork.

But everywhere it's silent.

"They're all in the fields for the harvest…" Donta says.

"I guess so, too," Carlotta whispers back. "I was half expecting them to be waiting for us as we descended the hills… How far is it to the church?"

"The church is in the next village…"

"I still can't believe that we've not turned into two piles of dust," Carlotta continues, "I'm hopeful now, like I did something good for once in my life…"

"I share the sentiment," Donta says, taking hold of Carlotta's hand and bringing it to his lips.

"Do you get any urges to pierce my skin?" she asks.

He shakes his head and says, "Your skin smells of roses—unlike before. It seems we have a higher power on our side to give us a chance."

Both of them turn, and glance up, staring west where the sun is still visible as a blazing ball, but now with a light orange glow to it.

"We best hurry," Donta says. "According to the story told in the church, the permission has to happen *before* night sets in…"

~~~

An hour later, the silence of a small village is disturbed by a creaking gate being opened hesitantly.

Donta glances around quickly for anyone present near the church, but when he sees the only street of the village devoid of any people. He takes gently hold of Carlotta's hand. Before he walks onto the green pasture surrounding the church, he lifts Carlotta's hand to his lips and kisses her hand gently.

She smiles at him warmly.

~~~

# Donta Naughty

Unlike Donta's actions in a place familiar to him, Carlotta's actions were more cautious.

As a hundred-year creature of the night, she had visited no sacred ground at all; at least not in more recent times. She cringes involuntarily; she looks at Donta when his hand squeezes hers tighter—in a lovingly encouraging fashion.

"It will be alright..." he whispers gently.

She nods and steps onto the grass, and stands still for a few minutes, staring around at the graves present. She glances back at Donta, asking, "Whose graves are these?"

"A decade before I was born there was an illness in the region and many people died that winter," he explains and he points. "That's the grave of my beloved aunt, who was my mother's sister. The one beside her is that of my youngest niece, who died at the same time..."

"So no one here was... errr... like me?" she asks.

"No..." he answers. "Why do you ask?"

"I had heard a rumour about what they do with my kind..." she answers.

"I'm like you now," he says. "If they want to harm you, they'll have to do the same to me."

She nods.

"Let's find the padre..." he suggests.

She nods once more, but her eyes dart around one more time, showing fear has set in for her.

"Remember that you promised me..." she whispers.

"Remember that you swore—Which grave is your grandmother's grave?"

Donta points to his right and says, "The grave with the statue of an angel above it is hers…"

"The angel is beautiful," Carlotta whispers.

"My grandmother was a sculptor in her life," he explains. "The statue is the last one she created before passing away. She was famous locally for her work. I'll show you the statues that stand in the gardens around my house—tomorrow… alright?"

**Donta Naughty**

# Chapter Twenty-Three

Carlotta's hand swipes over her cheek quickly, showing her mood has mellowed somewhat, showed by her tears. The conversation dampened her mood from happy to a deep sadness. Donta reaches up, and he wipes her tears away with a thumb.

She smiles weakly at him and it broadens with his next gently spoken words, "Carlotta, I love you with all my soul…"

"I love you too," she replies. "Until you taught me the real meaning of love—I behaved so stupidly towards you. I can't understand how you can forgive me…"

"You taught me something, too," Donta says softly, "and it filled me with too much pride until I met you. I behaved with an aloofness and like I was better than all those around me."

"We taught each other..." Carlotta says.

"That's what is likely the key to our salvation..." Donta agrees, nodding once.

"But we still need a blessing..." she comments hesitantly.

"I know, but I've always been a hopeful person. I've always have been like that," Donta says.

"I guess you taught me to be like that, too," she says. "I never had met someone like before you walked into my father's tavern. Do... do you think he'll be alright?"

"He may miss you. Pretty sure of it," he suggests. "To be honest, I don't really know the answers to the quest, but we can ask the padre if he knows what might happen to him now because of what has happened to you..."

Carlotta looks away, looking pensive, and she's silent for several minutes before she turns back to Donta, and comments, "The influence of—well, of me being a creature of the night—it will disappear especially if..."

She doesn't complete the sentence and Donta can guess what she wanted to say but is too afraid to admit. She realises that there is a possibility of them never getting the blessing. If it never happened, they would each turn to a pile of ash when the sun rose over the steps in front of the church, which is where they would need to stand and wait until the sun had risen in the sky.

"I'm afraid too," he says gently. "I never have felt afraid before. I wasn't afraid when I followed you to the meeting. Or when the sun rose the following day. But words of the padre were, 'By God's grace, the creature of the night is granted one day of His blessing when she wins the heart of an innocent victim, but the blessing from a man of God *will* determine if it's temporary or forever' and yes, I'm as afraid now…"

This time, Carlotta squeezes his hand, and she lets go his hand and reaches up and kisses his lips gently. He responds to the action by embracing her warmly and lovingly.

They part a moment later, and they look at one another with equal surprise.

"Did you sense it too?" she asks.

He nods.

Carlotta places her hand over Donta's chest and shrieks, "But that's impossible…"

Donta copies her actions, adding calmly, "Yes, you too…"

"But… but… people like us cannot have a heartbeat. We lose our soul when… when…" she says, but she isn't able to finish her sentence.

"You told me that before I found you, you felt like a massive pain had gone through your body, right?" he states quietly.

"Yes, but I do not know what it was…" she protests softly.

# Donta Naughty

"Remember what I said when I quoted the padre's words. The words the padre spoke when he was relating the story to the congregation..." he continues. "Maybe this proves that the story has a foundation of truth to it. He said that, often, the most outlandish stories have a basis of truth to them."

She nods and says, "It seems a plausible reasoning... He sounds kind to me..."

"When I realised I loved you despite what you tried to do to me—" Donta whispers. "I guess it's when God's grace came to *both* of us. My sacrifice allowed for *your* salvation, and your love meant that I never became... errr... a proper creature of the night... like all the others we saw turn to ash in the morning sun..."

"You're right," she says. "Do you think it means it can save me from... the same fate..."

"I swear on the graves of all my family around us I wish you to be alive, safe and in my loving arms when the sun rises tomorrow morning," Donta says gently.

"I guess we have either a few hours left or it is the beginning of an eternity with God's grace blessing us..." she mumbles.

"I'm certain the padre will bless us..." he says hopefully.

She nods, and it brings a smirk to Donta's face when he realises that she's nodded more in the last few hours than she'd done in the previous two weeks since meeting. She was also so much more subdued now than before.

Donta leans forward and whispers, "We'll have an entire day of rambunctious behaviour ahead of us tomorrow…"

Carlotta's face cracks into a wide grin and she nods resolutely; this time she appears confident. She glances towards the church and says, "We were looking for the padre. It seems he found us instead…"

Donta follows her gaze towards the church door. He sees a cloaked old man standing near the door; with folded hands, an enigmatic smile over his face and exuding endless patience, waiting for them to approach him.

Donta glances back towards Carlotta, smiles gently. A moment later, he holds out his hand. She takes hold of his hand gently and looks at him with a hopeful gaze. She leans forward and whispers, "At least he's smiling. That's a good sign…"

Donta nods and smiles back at her and says, "He was always a kind man. Kinder than I ever credited with, but if he's in a good mood now, it may be a good sign as you suggest…"

# Chapter Twenty-Four

Donta and Carlotta walk side by side towards the church door. Once they arrive at the door, the padre nods first at Donta and next he nods at Carlotta, who stands shyly next to Donta, hiding away from any possible scrutinising gazes from the padre. He reciprocates it by smiling at her invitingly.

"Welcome to my humble church," the padre says. "How are you faring, young Donta? I haven't seen you here for many months. I was told you followed in the footsteps of your dear cousin, is that correct?"

"That's correct, padre," Donta answers.

"And who is your companion?"

"This is my sweet Carlotta," Donta continues, pushing Carlotta forward. She protests for a few seconds, but she relaxes and steps forward with more confidence. She smiles at the padre.

"I welcome you to my humble church, dear child," the padre says gently, and nods his head once. "My name is Padre Miguel. Please, enter please, dear child…"

Padre Miguel motions at the door of the church. Carlotta glances at Donta, who now nods at her encouragingly. Carlotta takes a hesitant step forward, stops a moment, but in a few strides she's inside the church.

Donta feels a moment of hesitation before he copies Carlotta's actions and for the briefest moment he feels fear deep in his soul, but a moment later, two hands grab his own. Donta doesn't know which shocks him more; finding Carlotta alive inside the building or her action of, once more, teasing him with her breasts. A shuffle of footsteps behind him causes him to yank his hands away. She answers it with a light-hearted giggle.

"Why did you do that?" Donta hisses, but he notices no anger present in his voice.

Instead, he acts like he might have acted a decade earlier when he chased the scullery maid into the church and challenged her to have sex with him between the pews.

"You're not angry?" Carlotta asks; the surprise in her voice is clear.

"Of course not. I love you…" he whispers back,

eyeing the padre as he shuffles past them towards the altar. Not looking towards them yet, Donta feels like the padre is acutely aware of their presence and what they might do right now.

"Until he blesses us we need to be careful," he whispers towards Carlotta.

She frowns a moment - more from confusion than anger - but a few moments later she realises what Donta is referring to and she nods. She lowers her arms, clasps her fingers together elegantly, and somehow, she turns from an alluring woman to a demure girl in the blink of an eye.

"Is this better?" she whispers.

Donta smiles and nods. He realises now that, before the temptation had come to her to become a creature of the night, she was possibly an obedient daughter who'd cared deeply for her father, perhaps even was highly religious. Her pose shows that she's had the teachings from nuns.

"Were you at a convent for schooling?" Donta asks.

"How did you know?" she counters.

"I recognise the posture. My older sister had teachings at the convent in the east," Donta says.

"I went there before—" Carlotta says but she stops speaking, and glances towards the padre a moment. "Might he recognise the behaviour?"

"If he does, he'll likely look more favourable upon you…" Donta answers.

"One moment…" Carlotta says softly.

She walks towards a doorway next to the church entrance, disappears through the doorway there, and a moment later, she's back.

After she returns, it is obvious to Donta that Carlotta could easily pass for the daughter of one of the wealthier merchants in the nearby towns. She arranged her hair up in a tight bundle, draped over with a thin black veil. She wears an additional veil as a drape around her shoulders, causing her breasts to be invisible from sight. The red lip tint is gone from her lip. Her face is washed. Her skirt is straightened and seems longer…

"Is this better?" she asks once she's beside Donta again.

He stares at her in awe and mutters, "You look so beautiful…"

"I guess that's a yes…" she says, giggling softly.

"Good enough for being my bride…" he whispers.

"You mean… you mean…" she stutters.

"God's blessing means for us to be wed…" Donta says softly, looking down a moment; now he fears a sudden outburst and scolding rejection from Carlotta, regardless of the subsequent consequences that could come from it.

But the rejection doesn't come. Instead, he feels a hand tug at his face.

He resists for a few minutes but decides he must

check her appearance in the end.

"If we should marry to get the blessing—" Carlotta says softly. "I love you so much. I want to live a life with you… if that's at all possible for us both. But if not, please, find someone else to love… like you had promised earlier…"

"If you disappear from my life, I'm vowing my existence to do what *he* represents," Donta says quietly, discretely nodding sidelong towards the padre.

"You mean you'll become a padre like him?" Carlotta asks. "That's not what I want for you…"

"It's my choice to make. Just as it was my choice to do this…" Donta says, holding up his blemished hand up with the palm towards her.

"I guess… I understand," she whispers. "They did not give me any choice in anything I had to do before—My mother had forced me to learn at the convent. When she died, my father forced me to leave and come help him. Even the vampire who'd sired me never gave me any choice—"

"But you *gave* me a choice…" Donta interjects. "You did this by teaching me how wrong I had behaved before meeting you. The padre knows this too. He can see I'm a changed person. He sees I've grown up, that I've become a calm person committed to loyalty towards a person to love. He can see you had an excellent influence on me. Underneath everything you were doing, you proved you had a good heart. That's what allowed me to fall in love with *you*…"

# Chapter Twenty-Five

Immediately, Donta realises the impact of his words. He glances sideways at Carlotta and she seems to contemplate the words.

Donta knows what sort of person he was before meeting Carlotta. He'd been nasty to women, and often would be gratuitous at pandering for attention until a woman would give herself up willingly and find herself in bed with him. What he doesn't want to admit to is that he had seduced a woman into actions that had found him being chased from this very church by a mellow Padre Miguel.

"I was terrible, and I ended up on the receiving end of my behaviour when—," Donta whispers. He stops speaking.

"… when you were seduced by me—" Carlotta whispers.

She hesitates a moment before she adds, "But I was behaving in the same sort of way. I was treated similarly, and you ended up on the receiving end of *me* acting out the very behaviour of what was done to me…"

Donta embraces Carlotta before he whispers, "That's the whole point of the story, and why he told it to a congregation that included a disobedient, unruly boy called Donta."

Carlotta breathes in sharply.

From her reaction, Donta determines she hadn't realised what a terrible person Donta was before she'd met him in her father's tavern.

"It sounds like we were equally bad in how we'd treat others in the matters of love," she whispers, looking down with apparent shame.

"That's true…" he comments.

~~~

"DONTA!"
~~~

# Donta Naughty

Donta and Carlotta jerk away from one another. Neither had expected the padre's voice to be this loud. Donta stares surprised at the old padre. He had never heard the man use his voice so loudly before this day. But there is no anger in his voice.

"You look surprised…" Carlotta hisses.

"I am…" Donta hisses back. "I've never have heard him shout out this way…"

"I'm curious about what he wants…" she continues. "Maybe he's waiting for us…"

"I guess so, too," Donta whispers back. "Let's go to him. I mean regardless of whether his calling out my name as rebuke or to start the procedure described in the story…"

Donta and Carlotta look at one another. Donta holds out his right hand, and she places her hand in his with a gentle elegance that again could mistake her for a woman from a more prominent household.

After a pause of staring at one another, they pace forward towards the altar where the padre standing waiting for them.

~~~

Donta's heart is beating hard in his chest as he stands before Padre Miguel. He can sense Carlotta's nervousness from her repeated squeezes of his hand. He doesn't dare
~~~

to move his gaze from the padre to check on her wellbeing.

"I know of your past, young Donta, but what is her history?" Padre Miguel asks, nodding sideways towards the woman beside Donta.

"She is the woman I've fallen in love with…" Donta says hesitantly.

"And your intentions are to wed her?"

Donta nods.

"I guess your intentions are equal, dear child?"

Donta glances towards Carlotta, now that the questioning is being aimed at the woman beside him. He sees a shy nod. Now the moment of judgement by the padre has arrived, she shows the shyness of an innocent woman. If they're here waiting for a blessing - without the additional 'conditions' bringing them to the church - she may have been seen as shy by nature. It tells volumes about the sort of person she was as a child a hundred years ago.

"Tell me about yourself?" Padre Miguel asks next. "Are they aware you are here? Are you here with their permission? You appear to me to be a child still…"

"I'm an adult and I'm here by my will," Carlotta says in measured tones. "My father still lives, but my mother died in unfortunate circumstances…"

Donta frowns for a moment. She'd never disclosed to him *how* her mother had died, but the pain present on her face betrays it was a painful time in her life, and that the 'being forced to work in her father's tavern' alluded to a not-so-enjoyable time. It shows now why she'd done what she did to make her father be witness to her status as vampire using her power of persuasion to keep her own father under her will, thus reversing their roles.

*She let herself be sired as a revenge of how her parents behaved towards her, Donta thinks. But why…?*

"My father isn't able to be here anyway," Carlotta continues explaining.

*She sounds bitter when she mentions her father, Donta thinks. Like he might be responsible for her mother's death. Is it possible she became a victim like Carlotta had planned for me? But if her father did the same, and she was born a hundred years ago. Her father is also a vampire… Is he the one who sired his own daughter after killing her mother?*

"My mother died from… from a disease," Carlotta whispers.

*Hmm, I know what this 'disease' is in reality, Donta thinks. Is she going to be truthful about the actual cause of her mother's passing? She has to for God's blessing to be granted to us… I realise now the truth of who and what she is. She's over a hundred years older than I am…*

"There have been *no* plagues in this region for the last two centuries…" Padre Miguel says quietly. "What sort of disease was it?"

## Donta Naughty

"I have to be honest with you, Padre Miguel," Carlotta whispers, "and I'm a… creature of the night. I was—my father caused *this* to happen to me. He died yesterday too, because I poisoned his gin, and while he lay on the bed I opened the window of his bedroom. If someone goes to the tavern right now, they'll only ever find dust on his bed…"

Donta stares at Carlotta.

She'd showed that she'd done 'something' to make it easier for her to leave her home with relative ease…

# Chapter Twenty-Six

That Carlotta might be capable of patricide isn't an option that had even entered Donta's mind. It means he was, in fact, marrying a murderer. Her only option was to get forgiveness from a padre, to forgive her for a crime she'd committed...

*But is it even a crime if she became a creature of the night because of her father's actions a hundred years ago? When her own father killed her mother,* Donta thinks. *Is she even guilty of a crime? He's guilty of the crime of killing his wife... to become a vampire. He forced the existence on Carlotta against her will. It was my self-sacrifice that showed her how similar she was acting like her father...*

"You saw the murder of your mother," Donta says

softly. "Despite your dislike for her—You didn't like that she'd put you in the convent but you loved her enough to be deeply saddened by her being a victim in an annual gathering to select a leadership a hundred years ago…"

Donta hears the sharp intake of air from Padre Miguel.

The truth about Carlotta is now out in the open; both from her admission and from Donta's confirmation of knowing about her.

"Donta, are you here because of the story I told you as a boy?" Padre Miguel asks.

Donta jerks back to stare at the padre. He is equal in honesty to the woman beside him. He'd already eluded at his own inappropriate behaviour in a private conversation, but now she'd admitted to have killed her father as a revenge for killing her mother.

"I was here that day when you found me between the pews…" Donta whispers.

"And?" Padre Miguel asks; darting his eyes towards Carlotta.

"At first I was convinced that I could simply go out and find a girl to be gullible enough to want to be my wife," Donta continues. "But when I met Carlotta—She's taught me a different way of behaving, and—"

"But he also taught *me* to be different," Carlotta interjects. "He taught me that revenge by making your own father watching a daughter seduce as many men as she could…"

"So, you are *not* pure in sexual matters?" Padre Miguel says calmly; seemingly unfazed by the discussion going on.

Carlotta blushes deep red and simply shakes her head, before she hastily says, "He taught me a different behaviour and—"

"I'm *not* pure in sexual matters either…" Donta interjects.

"But are you both pure to each other?" Padre Miguel asks.

Donta and Carlotta look at one another questioningly, suggesting each is asking of the other person: "Are you…?"

"I guess we are pure…" Donta mumbles. "If I compare our situation with the story, you told me years ago…"

Donta glances back at the padre and awaits confirmation from the padre to show whether he's right or wrong with his assessment.

"So she sired you?" Padre Miguel says. "Hmm, that's not something I had expected to happen to you…"

"She sired me, but she never forced me to give my blood up unwillingly," Donta says defensively while pulling Carlotta closer to his side. "I volunteered my blood even though she had planned to lure me… errr… to lure me to my death like her father had done to her mother…"

"How do you know that?" Carlotta shrieks with fear clear in her voice.

# Donta Naughty

"One thing he will tell you is that I was good in school," Donta says, nodding sidelong towards the padre. "Good, despite my unruly nature. I have him to thank for that aspect of my life to be proper. I learned from ancient stories where always there was happened to the hero. Always there was another reason for their actions. Padre Miguel insisted I'd tell him what the reasoning was behind the story…"

"Is that what you meant by your earlier words? When you said that stories always have a deeper meaning?" Carlotta asks, glancing from person to person. They nod at the same time.

"It's also the reason I realised you were deceiving me," Donta answers. "But the same reasoning made me realise I had a love for you here…" Donta points at the place his heart is located, "… and here…" He points at his forehead. "When you love a person enough, your mind will make it easier to see their character, and to see the true person. You're as honourable to me as Dulcinea is to Don Quixote. You are my Dulcinea…"

"Is he honourable in your heart and mind, dear child?" Padre Miguel asks as he places his hand first gently on Carlotta's chest, and again on her forehead. Donta sees her flinch momentarily each time she's touched. It's the first time that a man, other than Donta, had been gentle towards Carlotta and it made her shy.

Even more so, it was likely that Padre Miguel was becoming something like a father figure for her. It was a loving father figure that had been missing in the earliest days of her life. It was her father who had taken her mother from her, even when the mother wasn't as loving as she should have been. But like Donta, the padre recognises that Carlotta had learned from somewhere to be loving underneath everything that had happened.

"Everything you tell me I'll take with me to the grave," Padre Miguel says. "I will never reveal to anyone that you were creatures of the night. You have my blessing. But remember the story, young Donta… Ultimately it is the power of God's grace you need to appease. If you both have won his almighty forgiveness, I can offer my blessing… Not before his might has manifested itself."

Donta and Carlotta glance at one another, both looking hopeful and worried at the same time. Donta brings Carlotta's hand to his lips, and he kisses it gently.

"Tomorrow we'll know if *we* succeeded, my love," Donta whispers. "Tomorrow *we* will know if *we* are another strange story about vampires being punished by God, or if *we* are the beginning of the stuff of legend, that people will whisper about but that they will never actually believe…"

She nods, smiling broadly at both men.

# Donta Naughty

# Chapter Twenty-Seven

Donta sits beside Carlotta, who'd relaxed while they wait for the night to pass. She glances up and smiles a moment. She looks back down and picks up something lying beside her.

"When you mentioned ours could be a story to teach, I spoke about to the padre about it," she says. "He's going to tell it in the same way as the story he narrated to you as a child. I asked him to tell it as a cautionary story if we never get God's blessing, or one of hope for people in love and not able to be together because something prevents them from being together by their own choice. He says history is filled with so many of such stories and that many men and women will come in the future who will write new stories with a similar nature."

"That sounds like a worthwhile thing to do…" Donta comments.

"You may need to teach me the skill of storytelling," Carlotta says. "It's not… something that the nuns of the convent would discuss. They said that it was not what a girl of my stature should explore with her mind."

"I will teach you everything I know," Donta says. "If by God's grace we're here tomorrow, we will start with the teachings. If I don't know it, we'll learn it together. You have as much right as I do to become a scholar. Padre Miguel excluded *no* woman or girl from this congregation whenever he taught…"

"How old is he?" Carlotta asks, glancing past Donta towards the hunched back of the padre who was obviously busying himself with the many duties his role as a church leader brings.

"My grandmother and he were childhood friends," Donta whispers. "He took her passing hard. He was forbidden from loving someone because of his calling, but there was always some sort of affection between them, according to my mother. Affection that ran deeper than friendship…"

"But he is pure, right?"

Donta nods and says, "He has never betrayed his calling. When he said he will take our secret to the grave, he means it…"

"I hope he has enough years left in him still," Carlotta whispers. "I really enjoy talking to him. He feels like the father I should have had, but that was always denied to me…"

"He says similar. He says that fate offered him a

chance to have a daughter," Donta says. "He likes you. Even if he will never outright say it openly. He may pray for God's grace to be granted to us. I've seen him in this posture in the past if he would pray for something…"

"To be honest, it feels odd to me to know that someone would root for us…" Carlotta says, glancing another time at the padre. She cocks her head, and it's obvious she's trying to hear the prayer being murmured.

"Can you hear any of it?" Donta asks.

"Hmm, God's grace also means that more and more of the skills that made me a vampire are now diminishing," she answers. "Before, I might have been able to hear sounds from outside. Now it's silent around me. Like it might be for *him*… It must peaceful for him to be bathed in the silence of this church whenever he wants to pray to God…"

"But you say that you cannot hear him?" Donta asks.

"I guess God wants us to be peaceful," she answers. "Whether it's peaceful before the end, or peaceful start of a new existence as—I don't really know if I'm explaining it well, but this church gives me a feeling of peace I've never felt before…"

Donta looks around the familiar church for several minutes with a new perspective offered by Carlotta's words.

~~~

Donta glances back towards Carlotta's direction at the
~~~

directness of her next words, "I want to release you from your vow," Carlotta says, changing the subject.

"Why say that?" he asks.

"Because right now I'm filled with hope," Carlotta answers. "For the first time since I was a child, I have genuine hope in my heart. You gave me hope first when you declared your love to me. The story gave me more hope. And he gives me even more hope…"

Carlotta nods towards the padre.

"How did he give you hope?"

"You say he regards me almost like a daughter," Carlotta says.

"Yes, he said as much to me," Donta says, grinning.

"When you've grown up unloved, having a person telling you you can be their daughter gives hope," Carlotta says. "I like him. He says he likes me. It gives me hope. So regardless of what will happen to me, I want to hold on to hope…"

"You forgot one thing…" Donta says, nudging Carlotta playfully.

"What did I forget?"

"Redemption is another vessel of hope, according to all the ancient stories he taught me about when I was a child," Donta says. "Many of them are about people who lose hope and find it again later on for various reasons. Often in an act of redemption. It's one part of the story I always loved to read…"

"I'll make our story one of hope and not caution as I had planned," Carlotta says. "Regardless of what will happen tomorrow…"

"You mean tonight…"

"Why tonight?"

"He says we only need to wait until the moon has risen to its zenith…"

"Oh, yeah. Midnight is when the new day begins…"

Carlotta giggles, and admits, "I forgot that. I was under the impression that we had to wait until the sun rose tomorrow morning…"

"In the old stories, it's always about balance," Donta explains. "In them, it's often a balance between light and darkness that creates the balance. The sun and moon represent this balance. As the first part of God's grace happened in daytime, that means the second part happens at night by the light of the moon. Padre Miguel says that the sun represents the male essence in such stories…"

"Ah, so the moon represents me, the woman…" Carlotta suggests.

Donta nods solemnly.

# Chapter Twenty-Eight

Carlotta leans her head against Donta's shoulder and closes her eyes. He sees a wistful smile play over her lips. He hopes she can truly start a new existence in a few hours from now…

Donta's mind goes over the events that had led them both to this church and he realises that he too feels equally happy. He feels at peace even if his mind is worried about her fate.

*If there is a higher being listening to me right now, please forgive my transgressions. Forgive hers. Give us the chance… a second chance… at happiness. Especially her. Had I been living here a hundred years ago, I could have saved her from her terrible existence. She never deserved the harm that came to her. I want to give her the happiness and decency she deserves.*

Donta glances up with misted eyes at the window, now willing the moonlight to come sooner and for it to be a sign of hope rather than despair. He frowns when a moment later a cloud burst makes it appear like the last beam of sunlight blinks at him. He glances down at Carlotta and sees her eyes closed. He glances at Padre Miguel and his back is turned.

If Donta received an encouraging sign from a higher being, he alone is its recipient.

"Carlotta," Donta whispers.

She lifts her head and looks up at him with glazed eyes and a weak smile.

"I decided something…" he continues.

She frowns a moment.

"When we're married we should sail on a ship that are travelling west," he says resolutely. "We can carve out our own destiny free from any stories or enquiries about how we met or who you are…"

"I like the plan," Carlotta says.

"We would need to dress you up though," Donta says. "The sailors have many superstitions about who can and cannot travel on a ship."

"I've heard about it from some patrons who'd come to my father's tavern…" Carlotta whispers. "I always laughed them off without realising that my existence is tied to a superstition. I guess I learned the hard way not to be so dismissive… What would we be doing in the Americas.

That's what they call the land…"

"Explore it, befriend the local people, teach them everything we know," Donta says.

"And become a legend for them," Carlotta says. "I have been thinking and I'm now curious if they know about creatures of the night at all in the Americas…"

"I don't know. But we never need to tell them about us once God's grace has blessed us," Donta says. "If they don't know about our kind, we can live there safely without ever being bothered with questions. If I learned to be less unruly, my father had showed he'd give me half of my inheritance. My father also trades with the Americas, and he has said that he thinks the king is squandering the land's wealth. It won't be much, but it's enough to help us start over."

"I lived with almost nothing for a hundred years," Carlotta says resolutely. "I made it possible for my father and I to keep the tavern despite the poverty we endured. I can make one gold coin be worth a hundred if you let me…"

"That's why I suggested this," Donta says. "We're equals. I want you to have a say in our future after this is all sorted out…"

~~~

"Donta, Carlotta, it is time for the blessing," Padre Miguel's voice booms across the empty church.

Donta takes hold of Carlotta's hand and they walk
~~~

slowly towards the altar, and cautiously they reach out to the liquid in the stone-carved basin beside the pew. They look sidelong at one another. It seems it tasked them with one ultimate test of their devotion. They glance back at Padre Miguel, who remains behind near the doorway, almost frozen in place like a statue.

After they glance at one another, their fingers dip into the liquid at the same time…

"I see your devotion is equal and true," Padre Miguel's voice booms through the empty church.

Rather than making them jump, the words cause relief wash over them. They know now they have showed their purity and their devotion to receive God's grace and a blessing for sacred union.

"I love you, Carlotta," Donta whispers.
"I love you as well, Donta of La Mancha."
Donta smiles in response to the acknowledgement of his true status.
"… but to me you, in private you'll always be Donta Naughty…"

Donta laughs out loud.

Rather than the nickname sounding malicious - as it had done once - now it had a playful jest to it. Carlotta grins broadly at him, and he rewards her comment with a kiss on her forehead and he whispers, "You may do so at all other times as well. If someone asks their meaning, you can *tell* them it was my rambunctious nature in bed with you that landed me the name. It's true really. It's the first moment of rambunctiousness that made you decide on the nickname."

"Only if you're alright about it…" Carlotta whispers back.

"I am…" Donta says, grinning. "It is what taught me to let go of my unruly nature and become a man…"

For Carlotta to use his correct family name rather than what she'd branded with him weeks ago shows him how much she'd changed in a few days. The same was true for Donta, and he'd showed it to be very true.

*She's gone from the wild creature, who deceived, to a gracious woman worthy of the family name. It doesn't matter that she, like Dulcinea before her, has come from an impoverished origin. Even if the origin is unusual, unlike that of Dulcinea…*

Not that *any* of the story of his more famous second cousin matters now…

~~~

After a few hours of silently contemplating each of their futures, without talking for a time, they look up and see daylight turn to the dusk before nightfall would come. The first evidence of moonlight enters the upper window of the church.
~~~

# Donta Naughty

Donta and Carlotta stare at one another once more, both smiling broadly, both realising that the *last* of the tasks to remove the curse from them, has been fulfilled.

Well, almost…

**Donta Naughty**

## Chapter Twenty-Nine

The hardest part is yet to come for Donta and Carlotta in the last moments of their story of redemption. It's the forgiveness and recognition of their love in the presence of the higher power represented by this building, and their host…

Padre Miguel closes in. He positions himself next to Donta, dwarfing him in stature. He leans forward, and he closely examines each of their hands that are at the bottom of the stone bowl filled with the holy water usually used for baptisms.

Once, a long time ago, Donta had been held on this very pew to be baptised by this padre. This part of his childhood feels like an eternity to Donta as he stares, looking confused, at his hand that's in the water beside Carlotta's hand.

"Does this mean we can…" Donta asks, grinning broadly.

A nod from Padre Miguel.

"I *want* to get married now…" she whispers.

"Yes—it has to be done right now," Padre Miguel says. "Before the moon rises, and before the light reaches *that* window…"

The padre points to the lowest eastern window of the church and says solemnly, "The first moonlight is being cast on the bottom pane of the window right now. It takes three hours until the moon casts its light on the floor right here."

Donta and Carlotta both nod to show they understand the explanation.

"Let's start with the ceremony…"

Donta and Carlotta jerk up as the words are spoken. They walk to the padre and take their places in front of him; facing each other; holding their hands; occasionally glancing sideways at pursuiting the moonlight towards them at the altar…

~~~
~~~

# Donta Naughty

"I*now* pronounce you husband and wife…"

Donta and Carlotta stare at the padre for a few moments, and they stare at one another, and next they both stare at the western church window.

"If the curse has truly been lifted—" Padre Miguel says gently while he also stares up at the window, "… The texts I had the privilege to read in my more youthful days claim the breaking of the curse will manifest itself with your skin covering with a white powder-like substance that falls to the floor. After the moon casts its first light through the eastern window, we'll know if the process is complete."

"So, no 'kiss the bride' until the moon rises?" Donta asks.

"Not until we can be entirely certain, and you'll be certain only *if* the unnatural white dust turns *blue* in the moonlight," Padre Miguel answers, "The texts where I read about the curse are ancient, and there aren't many who have read them as the knowledge within them is considered, well, to be dangerous. It could cause people to see this curse where it doesn't even exist…"

"What was the reason you told me?" Donta asks. "Well, all of us.? All of this congregation…?"

"Something made you *too* curious," Padre Miguel answers. "Something about how you behaved would have made you *too* prideful for your own good. Pride isn't a good thing for any person…"

"My father always would say I was *too* prideful as a child…" Carlotta whispers. "It's one of the hurtful things I still remember from childhood…"

"The test of true love and devotion is often the hardest to conquer between two wilful people, and your… circumstance *will* have made it worse," Padre Miguel says. "We'll know soon…"

Before anything more can be said, a white powder forms all over the skin of the two cursed individuals.

Padre Miguel steps back several paces to put some distance between himself and the couple, who stare at him with growing worry on their faces. The sensation of 'judgement' from the master of this church being cast over them both causes them to draw strength from one another.

If they haven't proved themselves worthy of redemption, the effort of making certain that they got married inside this church will be for naught.

The story of the curse flashes through Donta's mind as he stares at the floor.

The two small piles of unnaturally white dust lie unnaturally still at his foot, despite the occasional draft passing past Donta's ankles. He guesses it has something to do with the dust…

# Donta Naughty

~~~

Donta and Carlotta take a seat in the pews once more, and he holds Carlotta's hand tightly. She places her head against his shoulder and sighs. Time seems to pass so slowly now when it matters the most…

Donta feels a nudge against his ribcage and he looks up with a startle.

He leans forward, and he stares as, slowly, the blueish light of the moon creeps forward. He glances sidelong at Padre Miguel, who'd appeared to sleep until just this very moment.

"Is it really happening?" Carlotta asks.

"It seems so," Donta whispers back.

They hold their breath as the blue glow reaches the piles and in the next few minutes casts it in a blue hue.

For a few minutes nothing happens, when something causes Carlotta to draw in her breath sharply as the white powder turns a bright blue colour.

The light is gone.

And a few seconds later, so is the dust…

Donta and Carlotta trail the dust as it seems to dance
~~~

through the air. But there is no wind...

"I think you can *now* kiss her..." a booming voice announces beside them.

Donta and Carlotta stare at one another for a few minutes, and she's in Donta's arms with his lips over hers. They stop after a few minutes and stare at each other...

"How do you feel?" Padre Miguel asks.
"Unburdened, free..." Donta answers.
"Happy, like I've not felt in years," Carlotta adds.

"It has worked... You're freed from the eternal curse that had made you *both* creatures of the night," Padre Miguel says. "I expect to see *both* of you for the baptism of your first born..."

Donta and Carlotta nod, not even asking how it will be possible to have a child after an ordeal such as theirs. They only know that true happiness and true love are now theirs to pursue whatever life may bring them...

"Tomorrow we'll go home *before* we'll leave for our long journey west, and our *new* lives away from everything here," Donta says softly. "However, first you'll get to meet my cousin, and Dulcinea, and everyone else..."

**The End**